# 'Was the urge to hold the baby again irresistible?'

'I told you...'

'She's so soft and warm and cuddly, so sweetly appealing. Makes your stomach curl, doesn't it?'

'I...' Jayne floundered. It was true, yet it was true of all baby things: kittens and puppies and chickens. It didn't mean she was broody for a baby. 'It's only natural to feel caring towards a child this young,' she said defiantly.

'Does your new career make up for the child we could have had, Jayne?' Dan asked, insidiously striking the raw feelings that had erupted through her last night. 'The baby *we* could have shared.'

**Emma Darcy** nearly became an actress until her fiancé declared he preferred to attend the theatre *with* her. She became a wife and mother. Later, she took up oil painting—unsuccessfully, she remarks. Then she tried architecture, designing the family home in New South Wales. Next came romance writing—'the hardest and most challenging of all the activities', she confesses.

Recent titles by the same author:

IN NEED OF A WIFE
A WEDDING TO REMEMBER
THE FATHERHOOD AFFAIR
CLIMAX OF PASSION

# LAST STOP MARRIAGE

BY
EMMA DARCY

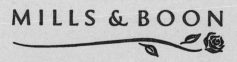

MILLS & BOON

To Guy Hallowes, whose interest in China
inspired our interest.

*MILLS & BOON and the Rose Device
are trademarks of the publisher.
Harlequin Mills & Boon Limited,
Eton House, 18-24 Paradise Road, Richmond, Surrey, TW9 1SR*

© Emma Darcy 1996

ISBN 0 263 79469 5

*Set in Times Roman 11.5 on 12pt
01-9605-43420 C1*

*Made and printed in Great Britain*

# CHAPTER ONE

'GET Dan Drayton.'

The plea ... the instruction ... the command ... thumped continuously through the shocked daze in Jayne Winter's mind as she watched her stricken employer being wheeled away, an oxygen mask clamped over his mouth and nose.

He had told her not to worry about anything else nor to let any other consideration get in the way. Dan Drayton could do the job. Given the critical situation, he would certainly take over and do the job for Monty. All Jayne had to do was contact him, brief him on the problem, and give him whatever assistance he required when he arrived.

Simple.

Except it wasn't simple.

Far from it.

Dan Drayton was the man she had married in blind passion and left when irreconcilable differences had formed an unbridgeable chasm between them. Monty Castle knew nothing about that part of her life. She had shut the door on it, asserting her independence by adopting her maiden name again before gaining employment as Monty's personal assistant.

Her estranged husband was the last person in the world she wanted to call on for help. She would rather be dragged over hot coals than admit any need for him whatsoever. As for working with him, being at his beck and call, having to carry out his orders...Jayne quailed at the thought of how Dan might use that situation to bring all sorts of pressure to bear on her.

Perhaps he was tied up in a contract and couldn't come. Perhaps he was somewhere inaccessible, impossible to reach. He had the soul of a Gypsy, his typically whimsical and eccentric ambition being to visit every country in the world in alphabetical order.

She had felt she was being swept away on a marvellous magic carpet when she had first married Dan. The magic had worn thin when she had found her life reduced to being a camp follower while he went out and blew up mountains or whatever else he was contracted to do as an explosives expert.

Iran had been the end for her, stuck in the American engineers' ghetto, going quietly mad with frustration. If she moved out of it she had to be covered from head to toe in black, a faceless person, a nothing person. That was how she had felt. She only really existed for Dan as the woman he came home to bed.

He was probably up to L or M by now. He had done China a long time ago so he wouldn't want to come here anyway. She hadn't particularly wanted to come to China herself, having done enough travelling with Dan to last her the rest of her life. Yet she now felt that in taking this trip and its accompanying challenges in her stride, she had really come of age as a person who could handle anything.

Dragon Lady...that was what the Chinese called her. It gave her a unique and individual identity and Jayne secretly revelled in it. Dan would undoubtedly put the name down as relating purely to her appearance, which, Jayne conceded, had initially inspired it.

With her willowy height and the cascade of fiery red ringlets that tumbled hectically around her face and shoulders, untameable by any hairdressing aid, she certainly stood out as unusual amongst the people of China. Her pale skin and vivid blue eyes increased the effect of being some strange, mythical creature, especially to the workers on the project site.

To them she was a subject of curiosity, awe, and a certain fearful respect. Being Monty Castle's personal assistant gave an aura of power, as well. Dragon Lady had definitely become an apt title for her, especially since she was so closely associated with and trusted by the explosives expert.

She had also earned it in her own right, Jayne assured herself. She had proved herself capable of carrying out any task that Monty had tossed at her with meticulous competence and efficiency. Handing her the responsibility of *getting Dan Drayton* was par for the course.

If only it was anyone else but Dan!

Jayne released a long, feeling sigh. It was no use hoping for Monty to make a speedy recovery. The forces of nature did not wait upon anyone's state of health. This was an emergency situation. The threat of a disastrous mudflow had to be stopped and that required an explosives expert who could move mountains. Monty had chosen Dan Drayton and he expected her to get him. She had to do it.

Her turbulent train of thought was abruptly interrupted by the arrival of Lin Zhiyong and his usual entourage. She had called him herself, requesting the best available modern, medical attention for Monty. As the highest ranking official, responsible for the successful completion of the new city of Denjing, Lin Zhiyong was well known to her. He was critically interested in Monty's protection plan.

Jayne didn't have to be told this was not a sympathy call. As the team of Chinese engineers who had been assigned to the project filed into Monty's office after Lin Zhiyong, she was well aware that she occupied the hot seat that Monty's collapse had created. These men wanted answers. They wanted direction and they wanted certainty in that direction. As Monty's personal assistant, it was up to her to fill the hole he had left.

Instinctively she stood tall, taking full advantage of her height as she greeted the much smaller dignitary and thanked him for his assistance in procuring fast, professional help for Monty.

Lin Zhiyong was well in his seventies. He invariably wore a Mao suit, apparently scorning the modern trend toward Western-styled clothes. Jayne suspected he was not comfortable about inviting in Western technology, either, but he was less comfortable with failure.

After a brief exchange of courtesies, he came to the purpose of his visit. 'It is most regrettable,' he stated without the slightest crack in his essentially enigmatic demeanor, 'but it would appear that Mr. Castle will not be capable of fulfilling his contract with our government in the time allotted.'

A broken contract meant Monty would take a huge loss, not only in personal investment but in reputation. Jayne knew she had to reply with confidence and authority.

'On the contrary, Mr. Castle will deliver on his contract,' she asserted. 'While he may not be able to do so personally, another expert in his field will take over and see Mr. Castle's plans to completion. Castle Constructions will finish the project on schedule.'

Lin Zhiyong stared at her with flat, black eyes, his timeless Chinese face as expressionless as the Buddhas in the old temples.

Conscious of the many onlookers in the office gauging her response to Lin Zhiyong's supposition, Jayne deliberately evoked the Dragon Lady image by keeping her shoulders straight, maintaining her full height, her head tilted as though she was about to emit fire from her nostrils, blue eyes ablaze with conviction.

The elderly official, however, was not about to be diverted from pursuing his point. He was too accustomed to a position of power over others to be overly impressed by a twenty-seven-year-old foreign woman, no matter how remarkable she was.

'May I inquire who it is you propose to call in?' he asked in a mild, silky tone.

It flashed through Jayne's mind that to hesitate was to show weakness. She had no choice. Any prevarication would be a terrible disservice to Monty.

'Dan Drayton,' she replied, not letting any hint of uncertainty show as she answered for her employer. 'He is recognised as one of the foremost explosives experts in the world. If you wish to check his credentials . . .'

'I am aware of his credentials, Miss Winter, as I am also aware he is presently occupied in Africa. It was the reason for our choosing your employer instead of Mr. Drayton in the first place.'

Africa! Was he in Liberia, Libya, or had he moved on to Morocco or Mozambique? Jayne couldn't think of any other countries whose name started with L or M in Africa. Dan might still be working through K. Kenya leapt to mind. Whatever the location, the more important question was, with what and whom was Dan occupied? If she literally couldn't get him...

'You do appreciate,' Lin Zhiyong went on, 'that time is an important factor in the contract.'

The softness of his tone did not veil the implacable intent in his words. There would be no extension of the deadlines to be met. Penalty clauses would be actioned.

Jayne had a few seconds of intense trepidation. Was it better to put damage control in place now? Were Monty's instructions a straw he was grasping at in a moment of great crisis, a straw that could prove more costly in the end? Or was she looking for a way out of having any personal contact with Dan?

One thing she wasn't, was a coward!

'I believe Mr. Drayton will oblige Mr. Castle in this matter. He will come,' she declared, trusting that Monty knew more than she did about Dan's present professional life. 'He will come,' she repeated with decisive assurance.

'You cannot know that,' Lin Zhiyong replied, unmoved from his sceptical viewpoint.

'I do know it,' Jayne retorted, stonewalling as hardily as General Jackson.

'How?'

The knowing challenge warned Jayne he was aware that she had not yet communicated the news of Monty's collapse to anyone outside China. The necessity to save face left her with no other option but to reveal a personal connection.

'Because Dan Drayton promised me I only had to call him for anything, and he would supply it.'

She had never put that promise to the test. She didn't doubt Dan had meant it at the time. He had wanted to show himself generous in their parting. Whether he would hold to it now after two years of silence from her was highly doubtful, but Lin Zhiyong couldn't know that.

She sensed a subtle change of attitude in the man confronting her, a flicker of recognition in his eyes acknowledging a different kind of power to his, a power that was essentially female. Dragon Lady could breathe fire into a man. The fire of desire.

The irony of it twisted Jayne's heart. That had been true between her and Dan throughout most of their marriage, but Dan wouldn't come to Monty's aid, if he came at all, because he still wanted her. Their desire for each other had wilted into insubstantial smoke under the deadening effect of other needs.

Nevertheless, she saw no reason to disillusion Lin Zhiyong's typically male deduction. It gave her the breathing space she needed.

'Today is the eighth day of the eighth lunar month,' Lin Zhiyong stated portentously. 'On the fifteenth day, when the moon is full, the people in this province celebrate *Zhongqiu Jie*, the Mid-Autumn Festival. I shall be hosting a party that evening. You and Mr. Drayton are cordially invited to my home, Miss Winter.'

In other words, Dan Drayton had better be here by then, or else!

Jayne mouthed all the correct, courteous words of acceptance and appreciation for both herself and Dan. Lin Zhiyong departed, satisfied he had gracefully applied the time pressure that would keep Monty Castle's project on schedule or prove it was impossible. It also allowed him to save face and retain his position of influence and power in the government hierarchical system that was so important to the Chinese.

The office emptied of visitors and Jayne shut the door after them, briefly leaning against it and closing her eyes, fiercely hoping she had not just set herself up for an ignominious fall.

She had to get Dan for Monty. It was a professional call, not a personal one. She hoped Dan was of a mind to let private bygones be bygones. She was simply doing her job, following her boss's instructions. She would state the problem, pass on Monty's request, and keep everything on a business basis.

A sense of pride stirred. It would be good for her if Dan did accept the proposition. It was the ideal opportunity to prove she had become her own person, self-determining and strong enough not to be affected by Dan or the memory of their all-consuming relationship. That was another life.

She pushed herself into action, making herself a pot of tea and stacking a plate with Chinese sugar biscuits before settling at Monty's desk. Somehow she now had to activate the plan she had just promised. She steeled herself to the task and picked up the telephone.

# CHAPTER TWO

DESPITE the time differential between the countries, various communication problems with officialdom, and a lot of persuasive effort on her part, Jayne tracked Dan Drayton to an apartment in Casablanca.

The long hours of tension, of holding herself together until her goal was reached, resulted in a sense of light-headedness when she heard the receiver of his telephone lifted from its cradle.

'Mmmh?'

Had she done it, or hadn't she? 'Am I speaking to Dan Drayton?' she asked, her voice almost cracking under the pressure of her need to know.

'Mmmh...'

It was a lazy, disinterested sound, but definitely not negative. Maybe she had woken him from a nap. An afternoon siesta was common in Mediterranean countries such as Morocco. Jayne took a deep breath, trying to calm the quickened tempo of her heartbeat. This was a terribly important business call. She had to get it right.

'Dan...' She hesitated. How would he react to her name? Irrelevant, she decided. 'Dan, it's Jayne. Jayne Winter. Your ex-wife.'

Ex-wife wasn't technically correct since neither of them had bothered getting an official divorce, but it was factually correct. Jayne didn't think Dan would quibble about it.

There was a long, disconcerting silence before he answered. Then to disconcert her even further, he spoke in his soft, sensual voice. 'I remember. What can I do for you, Jayne?'

It brought back memories that pierced the shield she'd put around her heart. So many times he had said those words, wanting her to be content with him, not seeing or understanding her need to find some self-fulfilment. They never stayed in one place long enough for her to settle to anything productive and interesting.

But that was over for her. She had to take control of this call, forget the past. 'I work for Monty Castle. I'm his personal assistant. He asked me to call you on his behalf.'

Another silence. Jayne hoped Dan was taking in that this was purely business, nothing personal at all. She heard some indistinct sounds that suggested someone else was with him, but she was totally unprepared for what came next.

'It's okay, Baby,' Dan murmured. 'Nothing to get disturbed about. This is the Jayne who was with me long before you came along. Here now, you can listen, too.'

The soothing, sexy drawl had a mind-shattering effect. The indulgent tone conjured up a baby-doll woman curled up to him, their heads sharing the same pillow. Jayne couldn't bear to dwell on what other level of intimacy they were sharing.

It didn't help at all to tell herself it was only natural for Dan to have found some other woman, or any number of them, to ease his sexual needs. She didn't want to hear the evidence of it. She remembered all too well how voracious his need for her had been when they were first married.

And for him to have told this current woman about her, about their marriage, felt like the worst kind of betrayal. What they had shared was private. Couldn't he have left it that way? As she had?

'So what's the problem, Jayne?'

She gritted her teeth and forced her mind back on to business. 'We're in China,' she blurted out, defensively emphasising the distance between them.

'Fascinating country.'

'Mr. Castle was called in as a consultant on the new Denjing city project.'

'I know.'

Had the two men discussed it? Perhaps Dan had recommended Monty after he himself had turned the contract down. Was that why Monty had chosen Dan to replace him?

'The construction could be threatened by a mudflow,' she hurried on.

'Nasty things, mudflows.'

'The threat has to be diverted,' Jayne explained, struggling to get her thoughts focused on the main issue.

'The right explosives in the right place. Simple.'

If only it was! Jayne took a deep breath, savagely berating herself for feeling so unreasonably...distracted...at discovering Dan was occupied with a woman on a level that was certainly not strictly business.

'A few big booms. That's what you like best, isn't it, Baby?' he went on, evoking a spluttering that sounded like a smothered giggle.

Jayne was not amused. Monty could be in danger of having another stroke, a fatal one, while Dan Drayton was playing stupid games with his *Baby*. Although to be fair, he couldn't know how tasteless this conversation was until she told him.

'Monty Castle had a stroke a few hours ago,' she stated bluntly.

Another silence. A sobered silence, Jayne hoped, fiercely clamping down on the stupid churning stirred by Baby's intrusive presence. Dan was entitled to do whatever he wanted. She had claimed the same right. It was just that it was...demeaning to be replaced by some brainless bimbo.

'How bad?' came the serious question, his voice deeper, sharper, driving her wandering mind back to the horror of Monty's grey face and stricken body. She desperately hoped the effects of the stroke would not last long. Monty was only in his fifties and one of the most vital people she had ever met.

'I don't know,' she answered, her concern for him uppermost as she explained further. 'He was still conscious and talking when he was taken to the hospital, but he'd lost control of his left side. He asked me to contact you. He said you'd take over the consultancy for him and fulfil the contract.'

There! It was all said now. How Dan reacted and responded was entirely up to him. She had done her part. Although a niggle of conscience told her she could do more. And should do more if more was needed to get Dan here. It was not only for Monty's sake. Lin Zhiyong had to be satisfied, as well.

'Give me your location and the name of the hospital.'

She complied with the demands, bridling at the thought that Dan intended to check the facts she had given him before making a decision. His next statement stunned her.

'I'll get there as soon as possible.'

For a moment, Jayne couldn't take it in. Dan was coming. Just like that. Just as Monty said he would. The assurance should have lifted a huge burden off her shoulders but it didn't. She felt the pressure of her mettle being tested, and Dan wasn't even here yet. It took an enormous effort of willpower to rise above the uneasy prospect of coming face-to-face with him again and concentrate on the more immediate problems to be resolved.

'How soon will that be?' She was amazed at how matter-of-fact she sounded.

'Mmmh... a little tricky. I was about to close a deal with Sheikh Omar El Talik, whom I don't care to offend.'

He could offer Baby as a candidate for the sheikh's harem, Jayne thought, then silently castigated herself for the shockingly sexist idea. She excused herself on the grounds that she needed Dan Drayton without any other ties. Monty needed him, she swiftly corrected, frowning over her muddled thinking. The faster Dan could come and go, the better.

'We should be there within a week,' came the considered estimate.

That made things easier. Lin Zhiyong's seven-day limit could be met. 'That's great! Thank you.'

She quickly explained the concerns of the Chinese official and passed on the invitation to the festival party, privately congratulating herself on coming to grips with the situation with growing aplomb.

'We'll be there,' Dan Drayton assured her decisively.

The repetition of *we* finally sank in. 'Are you bringing someone with you?'

'Baby goes everywhere with me. Wouldn't dream of leaving you with anyone else, would I, cuddlepie?'

Another bubbly splutter.

It was sickening. A ghastly vision leapt into Jayne's mind; a simpering nymphet clinging onto Dan's arm as he surveyed the mudflow problem with a bevy of intense Chinese engineers.

'There isn't going to be much time for entertainment once you're here on the job,' she warned, her mouth tightening, her stomach tightening at the thought of him turning up at Lin Zhiyong's party with another woman. How on earth would she save face in those circumstances?

'Don't worry about Baby. I'll look after her. Just book us a room in the best hotel there is in Xi'an.'

'It isn't five star international,' she said tartly. Surely Dan couldn't be serious about a woman he called *Baby*.

'I don't expect Baby will notice. A roof over her head, food to eat, me to love her...'

A bed was probably the only requirement, Jayne thought waspishly. 'Could you please send a confirming fax of your agreement to take over from Mr. Castle? It will prevent any problems from developing here.'

'Give me your fax number.'

She did so, trying to quell her irritation that he would not be as single-minded as she in com-

pleting the project for Monty. If Baby caused
complications or delays... Jayne shook her head.
She had no choice but to accept the situation and
do what she could to circumvent any distractions
from getting the project completed on schedule.

'Which way will you be coming in?' she asked.
'From Tokyo or Hong Kong?'

'On Dragon Air from Hong Kong.'

'I'll have someone waiting for you at Hong
Kong airport with the necessary visas, letters, et
cetera for entry.'

'Thank you, Jayne.'

Her skin prickled at the sensual caress in his
voice. She had forgotten how he could evoke responses like that simply with an expressive change
of tone. It was something she would have to
guard against.

She should probably ask for Baby's name, but
it could be filled in on the paperwork before the
flight into China. If it was something like Peach
Bubbles, she would probably throw up.

'Please keep me posted on your journey,' she
said stiffly. 'I'll be at Xi'an airport to meet you.'

'No need for that. We'll see you at Lin
Zhiyong's party. Baby and I will look forward
to it.'

A heated breath hissed between Jayne's teeth.
How could any woman stand being spoken of in
such a patronising manner? Did having a free
meal and travel ticket compensate for such de-
meaning paternalism? Was Baby's brain dulled

by a sexual drive that consumed any rational thought?

'Is there anything else you want done before you arrive here?' she asked, keeping her tone crisp and level. 'Mr. Castle instructed me to give you every assistance with the job.'

'Yes, I thought he would. Is that hard for you, Jayne?'

'Not at all,' she tossed off as blithely as she could.

'I wouldn't want to make your life miserable again.'

'Different circumstances, aren't they?' she grated, furious that he would imply such a thing in front of the woman he was bringing with him.

'Of course,' he agreed. 'Then we shall meet once more under a full moon. As I recall, the Mid-Autumn Festival is celebrated when the moon is at its fullest and brightest.'

The line was disconnected before she could make a comeback. Not that she had one. Better not to acknowledge the memory he had evoked anyway. It was in absolutely rotten taste for him to allude to the heady romance of their very first meeting when he was not only carrying on an intimate affair with another woman, but escorting that woman to Lin Zhiyong's full-moon party!

She crashed the receiver down on its cradle and glared at it with gathering turbulence. Her lips compressed. Dan Drayton had better keep his mind completely focused on work when he was with her. As fond as she was of Monty, her loyalty to him did not extend to tolerating insidious remarks about the past. If Dan Drayton once tried to put anything on her that was inappropriate to the situation, he would get a demonstration of Dragon Lady the like of which no one had ever seen before!

The fax machine signalled an incoming message. Jayne pushed herself to her feet and crossed the office to watch the transmission roll out. It was the official confirmation she had requested for the purpose of satisfying Lin Zhiyong and the team of Chinese engineers that the replacement expert was on his way.

The prime objective had been attained.

She had, indeed, got Dan Drayton.

The only question was whether she would get past this encounter, unscarred, unscathed and unhitched from the man she had once thought she would love forever.

# CHAPTER THREE

DRAGON LADY...

The name the Chinese had given his wife—she wasn't *ex* yet—simmered in Dan Drayton's mind as Lin Zhiyong's official car transported him and Baby from the hotel to this evening's party. It put Dan more and more in a dragon-slaying mood.

The Chinese might find Jayne formidable. He didn't. She could throw out as much fire as she liked. It couldn't match the slow burn that had been building in intensity inside him ever since her call. The desire to cut the wind out from under her wings and bring her thumping down to earth was uppermost on his agenda.

Jayne *Winter*. The denial of his name stung. She had been happy enough to be Jayne Drayton when they were first married. Throwing her maiden name at him was like saying their marriage had never been, scrubbing out the four years they had shared together as though it was nothing to her. *He* was nothing to her.

That was precisely how she had spoken to him, not the slightest acknowledgement of what they had once meant to each other, not even a civil inquiry about how he was or where he'd been or what he was doing now. What had he ever done to her to deserve being treated as though she had never had any personal, let alone intimate involvement with him?

It riled him even more that she had left him and gone to work for Monty Castle. If she had found sharing his life so intolerable, why had she become personal assistant to a man in the same line of work? And here she was in China, apparently contending easily with a culture that was every bit as foreign as that of Iran.

Baby pointed excitedly to the colourful paper lanterns strung from the trees in the park they were passing. It was a perfect evening and the park was thronged with people out to enjoy the festivities with their families and friends. Traditionally *Zhongqiu Jie* had always been 'the Reunion Festival', an occasion for the expression of nostalgic sentiments.

Dan wondered if Jayne knew that. The irony of it certainly struck him. The only reason for this reunion was Monty Castle's need for him. Dan didn't anticipate hearing any nostalgic sentiments from Jayne tonight, but he sure as hell intended to stir some memories.

It was a quixotic twist of fate that these circumstances had arisen. He'd never told Jayne his connection to Monty Castle. By the time they'd met and married, he'd gone way beyond being Monty's protégé in the explosives field.

It must have come as a heart-thumping shock when Monty had told her to get him. Though not so much of a shock that she had spilled the fact she was his wife. Monty still didn't know. That was obvious from their conversation at the hospital this afternoon.

It added another burning question to all the others in Dan's mind, making him pause before committing himself to helping Monty. A decision on the project could wait until he knew all he needed to know. In a professional sense, he'd already repaid Monty for all he'd learnt from him. He didn't owe him anything, except the caring that came with mutual liking. As for Jayne...

He cuddled Baby closer, rubbing his cheek over her soft black curls, breathing in the sweet scent of her, taking deep pleasure in the innocence of her love and trust in him. She was his first consideration now, not Jayne, and he had no compunction in ramming that home to the woman who had so comprehensively rejected him.

It had given him a great deal of satisfaction to hear the snippy tone creep into her voice when he had made continual reference to Baby on the telephone. It meant that she wasn't as indifferent as she wanted to be. He hoped it would hit her hard when she saw Baby, make her take stock of all she had walked away from.

The car came to a halt beside a set of steps that led up to the gate of a high, decorative wall that undoubtedly enclosed the gardens of Lin Zhiyong's home. The driver alighted to open the passenger door for them.

'Ready to go on show, Baby?' Dan asked, smiling indulgently at the small, angel face that gazed adoringly at him.

She smacked her lips in a kiss for him and he laughed, releasing some of the tension he was feeling over this meeting with Jayne. Baby was utterly, captivatingly beautiful.

Eat your heart out, Dragon Lady, Dan thought, stepping from the car. He settled Baby comfortably on his arm and went to confront the woman he had once thought he would love forever.

# CHAPTER FOUR

THE aim of a Chinese garden was to create a sense of peace and harmony. At some other time Jayne might have been able to enjoy the ambience Lin Zhiyong took such pride in; the graceful fall of willow fronds into the gently meandering pond, the carefully cultivated waterlilies, the artistic arch of the bridge that serviced a splendid pavilion centred over the water. It was all a visual delight, but Jayne was too on edge to feel peace or harmony.

Any minute now Dan Drayton would arrive with his *Baby*. Lin Zhiyong had sent his car for them. It was an unusually hospitable gesture for him. It was really her responsibility to arrange transport. She hoped Lin Zhiyong wasn't playing some secret hand. Dan hadn't actually signed an agreement with Monty yet.

'I am to be honoured with a special guest this evening,' the elderly official informed her. 'He is travelling from Beijing.'

A higher official from the seat of government? Jayne refrained from comment, not knowing what it might mean.

'It would appear that Mr. Castle has competition for Mr. Drayton's services.' he added enigmatically.

More pressure on her to make good her claim that Dan would do as she asked, Jayne thought, hating the sense of being backed into a corner from which there was no escape, yet determined to play out her hand as best she could.

She smiled, exuding every scrap of confidence she could muster. 'Mr. Drayton has always been a man of his word. It is regrettable that your honoured guest will be disappointed in his quest. However, I am sure his long journey will be rewarded by your hospitality.'

'It is best that he sees for himself,' Lin Zhiyong observed, his eyes glinting over Jayne before drifting toward the ornamental gateway into his garden.

At least her appearance had impressed him, Jayne thought, fiercely hoping it would outshine *Baby's*. It was not that she was jealous. This was purely politics. Dan was welcome to some other woman in his personal life. She simply needed a professional boost tonight. Besides, it was satisfying to have an appropriate occasion on which to wear the exotic outfit she had bought in Hong Kong.

At the time of purchase, she'd had no idea that the glamorous evening suit could take on another meaning. She had seen it as wonderfully rich and

perfect for her height and colouring. Tonight it
had a special impact.

The jacket was highly dramatic with a design
of dragons in gold and russet woven onto a lus-
trous pearl silk brocade. The heart-shaped
neckline dipped to a row of five buttons that
fastened the bodice to figure-moulding tightness.
The sleeves were long and fitted, with the dragon
motif featuring below the elbow. The jacket
flared out over the hips, giving it a winged effect.
Below it flowed a beautiful full-length circular
skirt in russet silk, gold thread crisscrossing it in
a diamond pattern that made it shimmer like
dragon scales.

Jayne had added some complementary
costume jewellery; a gold mesh necklace threaded
with pearls, and long, dangly earrings of chunkier
gold, studded with pearls. The massed red ringlets of her hair formed a fiery showcase for their
glitter and gleam.

She had certainly turned the heads of Lin
Zhiyong's other guests. Dragon Lady was making
her presence felt tonight. But would Dan re-
spond with the respect she needed from him?

'Ah, Mr. Drayton has arrived,' Lin Zhiyong
announced, apparently picking up some signal
from the aide stationed by the gateway. 'You
will accompany me to greet him?' he invited,
obviously wanting to observe their meeting firsthand.

'Thank you,' Jayne accepted, maintaining her pose of absolute confidence as she matched her step to his.

How she didn't falter when Dan entered the garden was little short of a miracle. Her heart certainly stopped in shock, kicking painfully when it resumed beating again. Her mind locked, one thought only exploding within the jammed compartment.

Baby...

He was holding a baby...a real baby...cradled contentedly in the crook of his arm...a baby with the face of a cherub, chubby little hands waving excitedly, a rosebud mouth blowing bubbles as she gurgled her delight in the glowing paper lanterns strung around the garden.

A baby with black curly hair...

Like Dan's!

A baby that looked to be about nine months old, certainly less than a year.

It was two years since she had rejected Dan's idea of having a baby to give her something to do, to keep her happy in their marriage, to hold her with him; ample time for him to father this child with some other woman; the baby she had denied him; denied herself.

The baby was observing her now, wide-eyed with wonder, dark-eyed like Dan...and there was an ache of emptiness in Jayne's stomach, a heavy, dragging feeling in her thighs, a cramping in her heart.

Somehow her feet kept moving. Dan had come to a standstill, obviously having observed her approach with Lin Zhiyong and waiting for the formal welcome to the Chinese official's home. It was not until they were virtually face-to-face that Jayne managed to wrench her gaze from his child to look directy at the man who no longer belonged to her, and would never belong to her again.

'Hello, Dan.' It was all she could think of to say. Her voice was smoky, insubstantial, barely emerging from the sense of dead ashes, all that was left now of their former relationship.

'Jayne...'

The bare acknowledgement was spoken in a guarded tone. The face that had once captivated her with its entrancing mobility of expression was unnaturally still, highlighting the distinctive bone structure that had fascinated her when he was asleep; the planes of his forehead, nose, cheeks, chin, all seeming to flow gracefully, one to the other in a complement of strength, yct the soft sensuality of his mouth hinting at a poetic soul that was at odds with the tensile power of his long, lean body.

His dark eyes clashed briefly with hers before turning to their host, and Jayne was left with a disturbing impression of deep, smouldering anger. She performed the ritual introductions with passable aplomb, yet she was acutely aware of a pins-and-needles sensation firing through her body, an instinctive alert to danger.

Despite the baby, despite whatever he shared with its mother, Dan Drayton was no more in-different to this situation than she was, and ex-ploding mountains was not the only explosion he had in mind. The life she had crafted without him was on a short fuse. She would have to tread very carefully once she was alone with him.

# CHAPTER FIVE

DAN was so used to dealing with officials in foreign countries, Lin Zhiyong presented no problem to him. He exchanged the proper courtesies with the appropriate amount of respect, and Jayne had to admire his deft charm in side-stepping some subtly probing questions from their wily host. Dan was giving nothing away, not his private nor his professional motives for being here.

Having gained no useful information whatsoever, Lin Zhiyong found his presence required by other guests and moved away to observe what transpired between Dan and Jayne at a distance. Jayne had privately decided that if she stuck rigidly to business she was on safe ground.

'Shall we stroll around the pond?' Dan suggested, taking the initiative from her with consummate ease. 'It will entertain Baby. I trust we have some leisure time for entertaining Baby this evening.'

Jayne felt a flush scorching up her neck and quickly half turned to accompany him side-by-side. If he hadn't exactly misled her about Baby when she had called him, he had certainly not laid out the truth for her. Nevertheless, she hated the feeling of being in the wrong, hated even more Dan driving it home to her.

'I didn't realise that Baby was actually a baby,' she admitted, wanting to clear the decks between them. 'When I called you I was still in shock from Monty's collapse.'

'Monty now, is it? You called him Mr. Castle on the phone.'

'I didn't know how well you knew him.'

'How well do *you* know him?'

The pointed question startled her into glancing at him. His gaze locked onto hers, holding it. He looked dark and dangerous, his eyes glittering with savage mockery. She stopped walking and confronted him face-on, deeply insulted by what he was implying.

'Are you asking if I'm sleeping with a man who's old enough to be my father?' she demanded, her own eyes projecting twin bolts of blue lightning to sizzle that idea out of his brain.

'It's been done by many a younger woman than you, Jayne. They usually have one thing in common.' His gaze raked her from head to foot. 'They're magnificently dressed and dripping with jewellery.'

Jayne almost stamped her foot in outrage at his horribly false interpretation of her dressing tonight. 'I bought this outfit myself,' she declared, breathing fire. 'In Hong Kong where we had a few days' stopover before coming on here.

And the jewellery is costume jewellery, which I also bought myself.'

'It must have cost a lot.'

'I earn a lot. And Monty Castle is my boss. Nothing more.'

'An extremely generous boss.'

'He happens to value me very highly, which is more than you did. I'm good at what I do.'

'You always were.'

'If you think that after you...' She stopped, appalled at having been goaded so far.

'Do go on, Jayne,' he invited silkily. 'You hold me fascinated. Are you implying that marriage to me put you off men altogether?'

No. There simply hadn't been anyone with Dan's sexual magnetism. Not for her. Dressed in a formal dinner suit, as he was tonight, he was as lethally attractive as ever, and Jayne was swamped with the feeling she would never really want any other man.

The reverse obviously wasn't true for Dan. She reminded herself forcefully of that by looking straight at the child he'd had with another woman. 'Where's the baby's mother?' she asked point-blank. If he wanted to talk lovers, let him answer to her!

'She died soon after Baby was born.'

Jayne's fire wilted. 'I'm sorry.' The words tripped out automatically, with no real sincerity. She was plunged into a state of confusion, pain mixed with relief, guilt, shame...

Here was a little baby girl, robbed of her mother virtually from birth. It was terribly, terribly wrong to feel glad the woman was permanently out of Dan's life. It wasn't as if she wanted to resume life with Dan, certainly not on the same terms as before. Besides, for all she knew, he could have formed another relationship by now. There might be more babies on the way!

This one didn't look uncared for. In fact she was beautifully, lovingly dressed in festival clothes. She wore a gold silk tunic with a little Mandarin collar. Underneath it were long pants in scarlet silk. There were beaded gold slippers on her tiny feet and scarlet ribbons tied around her head. She appeared to be as much adored and cherished as Chinese babies were by their parents.

'Do you have someone to help look after the baby?' Jayne asked, pursuing her thoughts to their logical end.

'No. I do it myself.'

'Everything?' Jayne's eyes flew up to his in sceptical amazement.

'Do you find something wrong with that, Jayne?'

It wasn't what most men would do. But then, Dan had never been like most men. He was a law unto himself and the only way to deal with him, live with him, was on *his* terms.

'I didn't think you'd take a child this young into the field with you when you're planting explosives,' she answered.

'Why not?'

'Because it's dangerous.'

'Not with me.'

'The noise...'

'Baby likes big booms, don't you, sweetheart?'

'Boom-boom,' the baby crowed back at him, clapping her hands as a chorus.

Jayne gave up the unwinnable argument and resumed walking, mortified at the thought that Lin Zhiyong had probably witnessed that incautious little scene. She fiercely vowed she would not be trapped into any more personal conversation. There was nothing to be gained by it and it only inflamed the heartburn that was eroding the composure it was vitally important for her to keep.

Dan wasn't about to change his rootless way of life. He was even bringing up his child to accept it as normal, carting her with him everywhere as though she didn't need anything but him. If she didn't, it made nonsense of Jayne's contention that children required a proper home base to give them a sense of security. Was Dan proving a point to her? Was that why he had come?

She mentally shook her head. It was far too extreme, even for Dan, to fly from Morocco to China to show her she was wrong. An infant didn't prove his case anyhow. Wait until Baby reached school age and see how she liked an ever-changing environment!

Dan had to intend taking up Monty's contract. Jayne felt compelled to pin him down to some firm decision before the competitor for his services arrived. It would not favour her position if Dan appeared to be weighing one offer against another in front of Lin Zhiyong.

'Monty told me you visited him this afternoon,' she began.

'Yes. He was able to curl his left fingers around Baby's hand. It's a good sign for recovery.'

'The doctors say his progress is very promising. He's well enough now to be flown home to Australia but he wants to settle everything with you first. Do you see some problem with fulfilling the contract?'

'No.'

'Monty said you deferred discussing it until tomorrow.'

'I like to scout a deal before committing myself to it.'

'What do you need to scout? You said the job was simple.'

'Other things aren't so simple.'

'For example?'

'Don't push me, Jayne.' The warning was spoken in a low, harsh tone. 'I'll do what I choose to do in my own time.'

It wasn't easy to quell her vexation at his elusiveness but she knew the warning was not an idle one. Persistence would irritate him, any attempt at persuasion would be treated with scorn, and she didn't have the power to seduce him from his self-set course. She had become bitterly resigned to that last fact before she had made the decision to leave him two years ago.

Their path had circumnavigated the pond and was now approaching one end of the bridge. Jayne looked toward the pavilion where most of the guests had gathered to enjoy the refreshments laid out for them. She didn't want to join them, not while she was still riven with uncertainty about Dan's intentions. She would probably choke on the moon cakes she would feel obliged to eat, especially since they were a symbol of reunion.

This meeting with Dan could hardly be classed as a *reunion*!

She felt sick with tension. Nothing was how she had expected it to be. She was sure she would have coped much better if Dan had been with another woman. That would have killed off any personal element straight away.

The baby really hurt. Dan as a devoted father hurt more. If she had stayed with him . . . no, she couldn't start thinking that. She had achieved something for herself over the past two years and she would not let Dan diminish that now. It was important to her to have an identity of her own, to know she was worth something by herself. Although the way things were going, Dragon Lady might very well end up a big fizzle this evening.

Baby pointed up to the full moon that was now dominating the clear evening sky and spurted forth a babble of baby pleasure that brought Dan to an attentive halt. He smiled indulgently at her, then turned his gaze to the object of her delight.

'If you look hard enough you'll see the lady in the moon,' he crooned softly.

'The man,' Jayne corrected, reacting sharply to being shut out of their closeness.

Dan slowly turned his head and looked at her with heart-twisting derision. 'You're in China, Jayne. Don't you know the old Chinese legend?'

Wherever he went he habitually asked questions of the local people, interested in their lives, their culture, their history. He picked up knowledge as easily as a sponge soaking up water. Jayne had never mastered the art, too wary of putting a foot wrong and possibly causing offence. For a woman there were many pitfalls in foreign countries that didn't seem to exist for men.

'I'm sorry I don't have your knack for drawing stories from people, and I don't read Chinese,' she said flatly.

'And you're too self-absorbed to wonder about anything outside yourself.'

'That's not true.' The criticism stung. Was that how he had seen her at the end?

'Isn't it, Jayne?' he retorted softly. 'You didn't even ask me how I was when you rang. You thought only of your needs.'

'Monty's needs. I was following his instructions,' she pleaded, realising for the first time that Dan had been deeply offended by her avoidance of ordinary civilities.

'You dealt with me as though I were a stranger.'

She couldn't deny it, yet she had deliberately used her personal connection with him to convince Lin Zhiyong that Dan Drayton was hers for the asking! Jayne squirmed with shame. Dan was right. He deserved better from her. Much better. They had loved each other once, shared many happy times together. To excuse her lack of any personal exchange with him on the grounds that it was easier not to remember those happy times did not mitigate the offence given.

'I'm sorry. I was upset. I didn't know how you'd react to hearing from me and I...' Her hands fluttered up in apologetic appeal. '...I just did my job, Dan.'

'Your all-important job.' His voice was a taunting lilt of irony. 'Has it filled every hole in your life, Jayne? Are you content with what you have now?'

'I get satisfaction from accomplishing things, meeting goals, seeing results. Is there something wrong with that?' she challenged quietly, aware she was treading on very thin ice.

He made it crystal clear he was on a low tolerance level with her. It might very well be her attitude toward him that would tip the scales either for or against taking over the contract from Monty. When he made no reply, she asked, 'What do you want from me, Dan?'

'The same thing you want. Satisfaction.' He turned his face back up to the moon. 'Legend has it that the lady's name was Chang Er. She was married to a tyrannical king. Did you find me a tyrannical husband, Jayne?'

'No. You were never that.'

'Chang Er was afraid for her people. Were you afraid of me?'

'No.'

'The tyrannical king came into possession of an elixir that would make him immortal. Chang Er realised his tyranny would go on and on forever. She saw only one escape from it. Why did you feel you had to escape from me, Jayne?'

'I needed a different life to the one you were bent on pursuing, Dan.'

She saw his jaw tighten. After a few moments he went on with the story. 'Chang Er wanted a different life, too. To rescue her people from the fate of being eternally yoked to such a king, she stole the elixir and drank it herself. The moment she had swallowed the last drop, she was transported to the moon where she lives to this day in total isolation.'

He paused, then softly added, 'I wonder if she still believes immortality was worth what she ended up with. I wonder how much she feels the loneliness of the long nights. Do you have an answer for that, Jayne?'

'She thought it was for the best and elected to pay whatever the price was. But the nights can be very long and very lonely,' she acknowledged quietly, regretting the emotional scars she had left on him.

'Do you think she would do the same again, knowing what her fate is now?'

'Yes. It was a matter of survival.'

'Perhaps it would have been an easier solution if she'd simply killed off the king. Wiped him out.' He swung his gaze back to her, his eyes glittering with hard purpose. 'That way she'd never have to see him, hear from him, or think of him again, and she could live as she pleased, free of any burdens he'd piled on her. Don't you prefer that scenario?'

'I think self-sacrifice makes for a better legend,' she answered warily, realising that he was lashing out at her for having completely cut him out of her life as though he had never mattered.

The truth was, he had mattered too much. She had been afraid of weakening if she kept in touch with him, torn between the need for the intensely passionate feelings that had tied them together and the compulsion to find her own feet apart from him.

'How much are you prepared to sacrifice in order to keep your precious job with Monty Castle, Jayne?'

So the gauntlet was down with a vengeance!

He wanted satisfaction.

The critical question was, what would satisfy him?

She could walk away from this job, just as she had walked away from him two years ago. That option was certainly open to her. But she didn't want to take it. There was more at stake here than a job. She wasn't sure she wanted to walk away from Dan again. Perhaps there was some other solution that she had been blind to in her desperation for a settled existence within an ambit she had some personal control over.

Her gaze slid down to the child, contentedly propped against his broad shoulder. Could she accept a baby that was his and not hers?

'What is her name?' she asked gruffly.

'Baby.'

'Not your pet name for her. Her Christian name.'

'I never thought of any other name but Baby.'

'For God's sake, Dan! She has to have a proper name.'

'What's wrong with Baby? She likes it. She responds to it. I'm not going to confuse her by calling her something else.'

'What about when she goes to school? Grows up? You can't expect her to live with a name like

Baby,' Jayne cried in exasperation at his stubborn obtuseness.

'The only nickname she can get is Babe. She'll be fine.'

'Only a man could think like that!'

'So I'm a man. She hasn't got a mother to give finer female consideration to a name.'

'Any mother would be tossing around names while she was pregnant. You must know what her mother wanted,' Jayne fired at him.

'I wasn't with her mother, so I don't know.'

'Why weren't you with her? It's absolutely unconscionable to get a woman pregnant and...'

'I didn't.'

'What do you mean...you didn't?'

'Baby isn't mine biologically. I inherited her.'

Jayne was hopelessly lost. 'You can't inherit a baby! No one inherits babies! Apart from which, you don't have any relatives to inherit from!'

He'd been an only child of parents who'd also been only children. His mother and father had been killed in a cyclone that had ripped through the Philippines. That had been when Dan was at university, studying for an engineering degree. He had been as alone in the world as she was when they had met and married.

'Do you remember Nina?' he said softly. 'Nina and Mike Lassiter?'

Nina had been her one friend in Iran, kind and sympathetic, although far more accepting of the hardships they faced. Before meeting and marrying Mike, who was an engineer attached to American relief forces, she had worked for World Vision in Ethiopia, nursing starving children.

'What about them?' she asked, aware that Mike and Dan had cemented an even closer friendship.

'They moved on to Somalia. Mike was killed in a skirmish organised by one of the warlords.'

'Oh, no!' Jayne cried in anguish for the loss of a man whose lifework had been dedicated to helping wherever help was most needed. It was clearing up after an earthquake that had taken him to Iran.

'I was in Madagascar,' Dan went on. 'Nina called me for help. She was close to giving birth and was afraid for the baby. She'd caught some virus that was going around and was weak and feverish. None of the medics could do anything for her. I think she knew she was going to die. She asked me to look after Baby for her. I promised I would.'

'Nina...' Jayne murmured sadly, her eyes blurring with tears as she looked at the baby once more... Nina's daughter...orphaned...with no close family to claim her and love her as Nina would have loved her.

Jayne's feeings about the baby... Dan's father-hood...were completely changed around. She was deeply moved that he had taken on the responsibility of parenthood with a generosity of heart that could shame many natural fathers. He had given his word to Nina and he was keeping to it, no matter what!

A man of his word.

That was what she had told Lin Zhiyong.

'Ah, Mr. Drayton, Miss Winter...'

Lin Zhiyong's voice! They both turned to see him making a beeline for them from the bridge. He was accompanied by a man in formal Arab dress. Behind them were two other men, similarly robed. The recollection flashed through Jayne's mind that Dan had been about to close a deal with a sheikh when she had called him in Casablanca.

This then was the competitor for Dan's services.

And she had not yet settled anything with Dan!

# CHAPTER SIX

THE moment Omar El Talik was hit by a full-frontal view of Jayne, he came to a dead halt. Dan winced. He knew what that meant.

First came the kick in the gut at seeing such a spectacularly beautiful woman. Then the mind snapped out of its initial stunned state and busied itself registering all the visual lushness of her femininity; the tumbled splendour of fiery curls framing her face and shoulders, the fascinating paleness of her skin, the womanly curves outlined and emphasised by the exotic jacket, the shimmering flow of her skirt with the suggestive image of long, long legs that could wrap around a man and offer him heaven.

That was when the tingling began in the loins, when desire smashed all other thought processes, when hands started itching to undo the buttons on the jacket and capture the full warm swell of her breasts, when the mouth went dry from the heat coursing through every vein, stirring, arousing, wanting like hell.

It was precisely what Dan had felt when he'd seen her walking toward him earlier. It had taken every atom of his willpower to appear unmoved, to retain his independence of her, to remind

50

himself that having and holding her was not on the agenda tonight, and the urge to kill whomever the man was who had inspired her to dress so sexily was not appropriate.

Dan felt a little easier about that now. Monty Castle was not a contender and she had more or less admitted to long, lonely nights. Maybe she had simply dressed up to feel good about herself. Possibly even for him. This last idea made Dan feel a lot better.

But Omar El Talik wasn't seeing anything beyond the impact Jayne made with her appearance tonight. Neither would any other man here if he had a full complement of male hormones. Dragon Lady had to be slaying them all.

The Chinese, of course, were never obvious in showing their thoughts. Omar El Talik had no such compunction. The hot desire in his flashing dark eyes was naked to anyone's view as he propelled himself forward again, eager to get closer to Jayne, touch her, woo her with all he had at his disposal. Dan's free hand instinctively clenched into a fist.

'Mr. Drayton you know,' Lin Zhiyong said with a graceful wave and a respectful nod.

'Omar,' Dan acknowledged, unclenching his fingers and holding out his hand.

He barely restrained himself from crushing the bones of the slim, brown, beautifully manicured hand of the oil-rich sheikh who had pursued him to China, still puffed up with the power of his wealth and unable to accept Dan didn't have a price.

'All is revealed,' Omar replied with arrogant certainty. '*Cherchez la femme!*'

Not as simple as that, old son, Dan thought savagely, watching with jaundiced eyes as the charm started oozing toward Jayne.

'Miss Winter, may I present Sheikh Omar El Talik,' Lin Zhiyong continued, completing the formalities.

Jayne's politely offered hand was enveloped by both of Omar's, his long, soft fingers caressing her skin as though valuing a precious piece of merchandise.

'I am honoured to meet you, Miss Winter,' he gushed. 'Never have I been so privileged! A woman who outshines the sun. You have entranced... no, enslaved me on sight.'

'Sorry to interrupt your enslavement, Omar, but I think I'm getting a cramp in my left arm. Would you mind holding Baby for a while, Jayne?'

Dan congratulated himself on catching her unawares, holding Baby out in such a way that the automatic reaction was to take the offered child. Jayne looked startled but she quickly settled Baby on her hip, balancing her there as though she had been doing it for years. Women's hips were obviously made to accommodate babies.

Dan shook and flexed his arm a few times to give veracity to his statement, observing with considerable satisfaction that Baby took up both Jayne's hands and Omar didn't have a chance in hell of continuing his seductive ministrations.

'It's a journey wasted, Omar,' Dan said coldly. 'I gave you my answer in Casablanca.'

'I understand completely,' came the magnanimous reply. 'And I assure you my trip is not wasted. I have not visited China before. Clearly there are opportunities for investment.' He smiled at Lin Zhiyong who nodded sagely. The smile sparkled more brightly as it moved to Jayne. 'And it contains a treasure that is brighter and more beautiful than any I have seen. You, Miss Winter.'

'You are very gallant, Your Excellency. Thank you for the compliment,' Jayne said without any marked enthusiasm. Which demonstrated she had not lost her good taste!

Baby reached up to explore the elaborate pearl and gold necklace that dangled provocatively above a shadowed hint of cleavage. Jayne gently prevented her from tugging it by guiding the little fingers over the beaded mesh. It was perfectly plain to Dan that Omar desired his fingers in the same place.

'You should be draped in diamonds, Miss Winter. And sapphires to match the flashing brilliance of your eyes,' he raved on, determined to recapture and hold Jayne's attention. 'To pay you the homage you deserve I would lay the world at your feet. Anything you desire, Miss Winter. All you have ever dreamed of.'

'I don't believe any one person can give another all that is desired,' Jayne replied with an edge of irony. 'Complete satisfaction is hard to come by. It seems to me that compromises always have to be made and men expect women to make them.' She looked directly at Dan, her eyes blue slashes of mockery. 'While they do as they wish.'

Dan gritted his teeth, biting down on a cutting retort. He hadn't deceived her about the kind of life he led and she'd been perfectly happy to marry him. It wasn't his fault she'd changed her mind about what would make her happy.

'You are right,' Omar agreed with fervour. 'You are a queen amongst women, Miss Winter. You should be in command of men. I am at your command. Ask anything of me and I will do it.'

'A new plan, Omar? Buy Jayne and you think I'll follow?' Dan interposed sardonically. The political need not to offend was erased by a primitive urge to smash Omar's suit to Jayne. 'Your father must be pressing you hard. Didn't you tell him I was no longer available to advise on his mining operations?'

Dark fury stabbed at Dan. 'You insult me. And you insult the lady.'

'Offering her diamonds and sapphires and all she desires is not an attempt to buy her?'

'It is a tribute to her beauty.' He snubbed Dan and turned back to Jayne. 'As you can see, Mr.

Drayton thinks of himself. I think of you, Miss Winter. My private jet is standing by at Beijing. I will fly you to the great fashion houses of Paris. To Amsterdam for the finest and most exquisite jewellery in the world.'

'You are very flattering, Your Excellency,' Jayne said, sounding somewhat bemused. 'But I do have responsibilities here.'

'There is nothing that cannot be rearranged,' Omar assured her.

Dan seethed with frustration. He'd been sorting Jayne out very neatly before this fly in the ointment had arrived. Jayne would undoubtedly get a swelled head out of these extravagant bribes even if she rejected them.

Unfortunately Omar El Talik had less of a stomach for rejection than Dan did. He might be an adult physically but he had the mind of a spoilt brat. He wanted Jayne and he was used to getting what he wanted, one way or another. Dan wouldn't put it past him to kidnap her. He had his two heavies with him. There was only one way Dan could see to spike his ardour.

'I don't take kindly to your rearranging anything for Jayne. Or me,' he drawled.

The implied threat only stirred a haughty arrogance. 'Miss Winter is far above the menial work of an assistant and she is free to choose. Apart from which, I doubt very much you would do anything to harm her.' His hot, dark eyes coveted Jayne again. 'Miss Winter...'

'. . . happens to be my wife,' Dan stated categorically. He glared a warning at Jayne. If she said, 'Ex-wife,' he would take Baby and walk out right now. If she ended up back in the Middle East, having to submit to purdah for the rest of her life, she only had herself to blame.

'I do not believe you,' Omar scoffed. 'Miss Winter does not bear your name.'

'Why should she? She has a perfectly good name of her own,' Dan argued, repressing his burning resentment that Jayne had chosen to eschew any connection to him. He smiled at Lin Zhiyong. 'It's the custom in China for married women to retain their maiden names.'

'It is so,' the elderly official agreed, nodding affably.

'She would have had the child with her,' Omar astutely pointed out.

'Jayne was busy doing what she wanted to do and I wanted the pleasure of having Baby with me,' Dan declared, reaching out to gently ruffle Baby's curls. 'I can recommend the joys of fatherhood.'

Omar bristled with scepticism. He appealed to Jayne. 'This is a ploy to keep you to himself, is it not?'

Dan tensed. This was the moment of decision!

'It was I who called him, Your Excellency,' Jayne replied with an emphasis that subtly drew attention to her own autonomy. 'His expertise is required here. As my husband, he promised me that I only had to call him and he would supply what I requested.'

The offer hadn't been meant for this situation, Dan thought in exasperation, remembering how he had anticipated a change of mind from Jayne after a few weeks' separation. He simply hadn't believed she would want to live apart from him for long. To comprehensively disappear for two years had been beyond any conceivable calculations.

He watched in glowering impotence as she smiled at Lin Zhiyong, exuding all her prodigious female power, then turned her smile on him, her eyes ablaze with challenge.

'I want Dan to fulfil Monty Castle's contract. You are going to do that, aren't you, Dan?'

She well deserved the name of Dragon Lady! He'd been doing the decent thing in trying to protect her from the clutches of Omar El Talik and she'd turned it into a neat piece of entrapment. Nevertheless, two could play at that game.

'For my wife, yes. I'm looking forward to our living together again while we bring this project to completion.'

Her smile stiffened.

She knew and he knew she couldn't walk away from him this time, not until Monty's contract was fulfilled. Dan relished the thought of taking every day of the allotted time to do the job. He had a lot of scores to settle with Dragon Lady.

'Starting tonight,' he hammered home.

Caught, Dan thought, and the sense of satisfaction that flooded through him salved much of the frustration that had been eating him for two long years!

# CHAPTER SEVEN

SERENELY triumphant was the pose she had to sustain as Dragon Lady, having accomplished what Lin Zhiyong had plainly doubted, but Jayne was boiling underneath it.

Dan Drayton had appropriated her as though she was a possession he could pick up and do anything he liked with whenever the whim took him. It was a timely reminder of why she had walked out of their marriage.

The feelings he'd stirred were treacherous. She couldn't afford to let him mush up her heart with Nina's baby. And he might be the most compellingly attractive man she'd ever met, but if he thought he was going to resume conjugal rights tonight, he had another think coming!

Two years she had spent trying to establish herself as a person in her own right. For him to claim her as his wife and expect to live with her again without so much as an 'if you please', showed a total lack of respect for her position and her feelings.

There was no immediate opportunity for private conversation. Lin Zhiyong proved himself a diplomat, smoothly breaking up the awkward impasse for Sheikh Omar El Talik by inviting them all to take refreshment in the pavilion, which, he pointed out to his foreign guests, was a fine example of traditional Chinese architecture.

Dan deftly relieved Jayne of Baby's weight with a smug grin that she would have liked to slap off his face. He hoisted the little girl to a perch against his shoulder again—no painful residue from the cramp in his arm—and was fulsome in his admiration of the pavilion's green-tiled roof with its winged eaves and the red-lacquered pillars and beams that supported it. The designs of flowers painted on the beams drew his particular interest. As an appreciative guest, Dan scored full marks.

Not so Sheikh Omar El Talik. He was sullenly silent, disinterested in any ornamentation that didn't have Jayne at the centre of it. He still cast hotly meaningful looks at her and was intensely watchful for any sign of disunity between the supposedly reunited couple.

He declined a moon cake, despite the variety of unique fillings Lin Zhiyong listed to tempt his appetite. However, he accepted a small cup of Maotai, one of the most famous Chinese wines, a transparent, potent spirit made from sorghum and guaranteed to take the fire out of his eyes and put it in his mouth and stomach. Lin Zhiyong failed to tell him about this effect. He emptied the warmed cup in one gulp and barely saved himself the indignity of coughing and spluttering.

That was the end of the party as far as Omar El Talik was concerned. He made an abrupt farewell and departed with his men. Jayne was glad to see the back of him. With Lin Zhiyong escorting the trio of Arabs from his garden, there was no one of importance in hearing distance of what she wanted to say to Dan.

He was feeding Baby little pieces of the sweet cake he had selected, much to her gooing approval. Jayne finished the cup of light rice wine she had taken and moved to the railing at one end of the pavilion, ostensibly to admire the reflection of the full moon in the water but practically ensuring a small pocket of privacy.

Predictably Dan followed, taking up position at her side and making an innocuous comment about the pleasing formation of the waterlilies.

Jayne turned on him, not even minimally pacified by the sensual splendour of the view. 'I do not need you to create diversionary tactics to rescue me from the attentions of other men,' she steamed.

Dan was not the least bit chastened. 'You preferred him mauling you?' he asked, as though miffed at her lack of appreciation for his quick thinking.

'I was perfectly capable of detaching myself.'

He snorted. 'You would have had a constant job of it.'

Jayne's temperature rose. 'So your judgement's better than mine, is it?'

'In this case, yes.'

She exploded with resentment. 'Thank you for reducing me to the status of second-class citizen, Dan. It reminds me quite forcefully of why I left you. The way you took over and answered for me as though I had no voice of my own showed a truly wonderful contempt for my intelligence and savoir faire.'

'Not at all. I'm full of admiration for the way you turned the situation to your advantage,' he drawled, completely unstung by her accusations. 'A splendid piece of opportunism.'

'Which you promptly capitalised upon. Or thought you did.'

'Now there you've lost me. You were doing the capitalising for Monty.'

'I do not sell my body to anyone for anyone, Dan Drayton,' she hissed, furious that he was ducking the point.

'Neither you should. I couldn't agree more.'

She barely stopped herself from yelling at him. With enormous self-discipline she bit out the bottom line. 'I will not be living with you.'

'Oh, yes, you will,' he said decisively. 'The deal's off if you don't.'

'If you think you can jump into my bed anytime you like, just because you once had that right . . .'

'Right? Right?' His voice rose in a scandalised squawk, drawing unwelcome attention.

'Shhh . . .'

He dropped his tone to silky sarcasm. 'Oh, that's lovely, that is! Reducing our lovemaking to marital rights. As though you weren't every bit as passionately involved as I was. Twisting the truth now, are we?'

Jayne flushed. 'So it was mutual consent then. It isn't now.'

'You can say that again!'

'I beg your pardon.'

'Just because Omar had the hots for you, you needn't think I'm panting to slide between the sheets with you, Jayne Winter. You froze me out for two years and you'd have to chip the frost off me and do a big heating-up program to get me even mildly interested.'

'Oh!' Jayne was so deflated she was robbed of speech.

'It's obviously going to be a pain in the neck living with Dragon Lady.'

'What?'

'That's the name the Chinese people here have given you. Undoubtedly with good reason. Not exactly suggestive of a comfortable person to live with, is it?'

'I'm not asking you to live with me. I don't want you to live with me.' Jayne heard her voice growing shrill, and swallowed hard, fighting to regain a calm composure.

'Part of the job unfortunately,' Dan said with a rueful grimace. 'Much easier and more efficient if you're on hand to assist with Monty's plans and projections.'

'We can meet on the job,' Jayne flung at him. 'There is no need for us to cohabit.'

'And what if Omar whisks you off in his private jet to have his way with you? I'd be left having to sort out everything for myself. The deal was for you to stay on the job.'

'Oh, for heaven's sake! As if that's going to happen!'

'Highly likely if we don't stay together with every appearance of marital bliss. Omar El Talik is not a man who cares to be thwarted. White slavery was once a popular trade in his country. And very lucrative. He'd have no scruples about taking you, Jayne.'

'This is absolute nonsense!' she scoffed.

'Don't let the diamonds and sapphires fool you. Even queens are second-class citizens in Omar's world.'

'Will you stop this!' Jayne cried in exasperation. 'It's not going to happen.'

'Well, you might be prepared to chance it. I'm not. You got me into this and now you're stuck with me. Take it or leave it. Here's Lin Zhiyong coming back if you want to tell him the deal's off. Of course, I'm now persona non grata in Morocco after this little altercation with Omar, but Baby and I are quite happy to travel on to Mozambique. We certainly don't need this aggravation.'

Having neatly established himself on the moral high ground, Dan adopted a lofty air of distancing himself from her decision. It stirred a maelstrom of violent feelings in Jayne. She dearly wanted to kick him. The almost overwhelming urge demonstrated how deeply Dan could still get under her skin.

She looked up at the full moon sailing serenely across the heavens and thought Chang Er probably had herself a good deal. In her lunar isolation she didn't have to put up with men!

Jayne was acutely aware she was playing with fire having anything more to do with Dan. Yet if she didn't stand up to him now, what was her much vaunted self-determination worth? If he was prepared to live together on a platonic basis, her pride insisted she could do the same. After all, it would surely be the ultimate testing ground of what they meant to each other.

Out of the corner of her eye, Jayne saw Lin Zhiyong stepping onto the bridge. There was no time left for further consideration. 'All right,' she conceded. 'We live together. Monty and I were sharing a two-bedroom apartment. You and Baby can have Monty's room.'

Dan favoured her with a look of pained resignation. 'I do hope it's not too cramped. I wouldn't want Baby to disturb your sleep.'

It wouldn't be Baby disturbing her sleep. Knowing Dan was occupying Monty's bed with only a wall between them was going to stimulate memories that were guaranteed to keep her awake and restless. His apparent sangfroid over the enforced proximity did nothing to allay her newly aroused awareness of the husband she had striven so hard to forget. She found it galling, especially since she had been unable to maintain any coolness herself from the moment of seeing him again.

'If you'd like to suggest some other accommodation?' she offered tightly.

'No. If it suited Monty, I daresay it will suit Baby and me well enough,' he said reasonably. 'I was merely considering you, Jayne. But if you're satisfied, I'm satisfied.'

She stared at him, almost certain she saw malicious devilment dancing in his eyes, but his general demeanour was stand-offish and he swung his gaze away from her as Lin Zhiyong arrived beside them.

'Is His Excellency travelling straight back to Beijing?' Dan asked.

'He did not say,' Lin Zhiyong replied. 'I am informed that His Excellency has rooms booked in the same hotel as yourself, Mr. Drayton. In Xi'an.' He hesitated, looking sharply at Jayne before addressing Dan again. 'You are not thinking of changing your mind over ...?'

'Most assuredly not,' Dan replied emphatically. 'However, I am intent on safeguarding my wife from Omar El Talik's unwelcome attentions. Would it be possible to arrange to have my luggage collected from my hotel and delivered here so that I can accompany my wife straight to her apartment at the completion of tonight's festivities?'

'It is no problem at all. Leave it with me,' Lin Zhiyong instantly obliged. 'And may I say, Mr. Drayton, how pleased I am to have your services in resolving our difficult problem.'

'You owe that outcome to my wife,' Dan said dryly.

'Yes,' Lin Zhiyong agreed, bowing in respect to Jayne. 'Miss Winter is, indeed, a lady to be counted.'

Dragon Lady.

Jayne felt a bubble of hysteria rise in her throat and hastily swallowed it down. Not only had she *saved face* tonight, she had probably increased it a hundredfold. Only she could taste the bitter irony of what was really going on.

Dan was taking revenge for her desertion of him, forcing her to contemplate at close quarters all she had given up, ramming the price she had paid for independence right down her throat. That was the truth of it.

As she considered the inevitable misery of her immediate fate, another truth rose above the churning emotional mess Dan had reduced her to.

Dan could not be as immune to her as he made himself out to be. It might have been curiosity and a damaged ego that had prompted him to come at her call, but he had come! And he had acted quite jealously and possessively in the face of Omar El Talik's zealous homage and extravagant promises.

He had been hurt by her ultimate rejection of all their marriage had meant and it could be pride that prompted his present stand-off with her. Maybe living together would give them the opportunity to air their differences and reach a mutual understanding. If he had suffered long, lonely nights, perhaps some kind of compromise could be reached.

Well, she would soon find out.

The trial by fire had already begun.

# CHAPTER EIGHT

IF DAN really wanted her as his wife again, he gave no indication of it as he moved his luggage into the apartment, checked the facilities and reorganised the space in Monty's bedroom to accommodate his and Baby's needs. He might well have been the stranger Jayne had made of him. There was no attempt to evoke any intimacy between them, nor to engage her in provocative conversation. He simply moved in with military-like precision.

There was no mistaking the message being telegraphed to Jayne. An invasion of her bedroom tonight was definitely not on Dan's agenda. She could sleep in lonely peace as far as he was concerned. Yet peace was as far away as the moon.

Loneliness wasn't.

Jayne lay awake long after all noise in the next bedroom ceased. The loneliness she felt was soul-deep. It went far beyond the separation from Dan, right back to her childhood. The sight of Baby settled in Monty's double bed, on the other side to where Dan would lie, triggered memories she had suppressed for many years.

If her own parents had shared their bed with her when she was a baby, Jayne didn't remember

it. She remembered sleeping on floors, arm-
chairs, sofas, car seats, never in a bed of her own
in a place she could call home.

Her parents had always been on the move,
going wherever the rock band her father played
in had a booking. Music had been his life, although the band had never managed to hit the
big-time. Hotels, clubs, dance halls comprised
most of their venues. The one constant Jayne remembered was the Kombivan stacked with sound
equipment and instruments.

Her mother had died from a particularly viru-
lent form of influenza when Jayne was seven.
Travelling with the band had stopped then. She
was farmed out to friends or relatives of the band
members, anyone who was willing to help, having
Jayne for a while. Neither of her parents had
family for her to go to. They had both been run-
aways from broken homes and de facto relation-
ships where they no longer 'fitted'.

Jayne hadn't 'fitted' anywhere, either,
although she had tried to be as unobtrusive as
possible to those who were kind enough to take
her in. Schooling had been erratic, but it did introduce her to the world of books and Jayne had
retreated into it at every opportunity. Naturally
good at numbers, she had picked up maths easily.
None of the multitude of teachers she had in
primary school ever seemed to notice any short-
comings in her education.

High school had introduced her to computers.
She loved working on them. It was something,
albeit a machine, that she could control. Nothing
else in her life was controllable. People came and
went, including her father, whose haphazard
visits usually meant shifting to another place,
another school, another set of strangers to put
names to.

He had tried to jolly her into being more out-
going, more cheerful to be with. A quiet, in-
troverted bookworm did not win friends. She
should try to develop more people skills, join in
with whatever was going on. It would make life
easier for her. After all, she was a bright spark,
he would say, ruffling the red curls she had inherited from him.

Jayne had figured her father didn't touch down
on the real world or didn't want to examine it
too closely. At the schools she attended boys invariably teased her over her tallness and her mop
of red hair. Girls had their established cliques.
Jayne was an outsider. She didn't reject whatever
overtures of friendship were made to her but she
knew in her heart that nothing lasting would
eventuate. How could it when next week, next
month, next term, she might be somewhere else?

She never did really learn people skills. She
responded to those who made the effort to talk
to her but didn't know how to go about drawing
a response from them if it wasn't readily forth-
coming. Dan had accused her tonight of being

too self-absorbed to wonder about anyone else. Was that how she came over to others?

Had Nina seen her like that?

Did Monty?

Jayne didn't think it was true, yet she couldn't deny the habit of distancing herself from any source of hurt. As she had done with Dan when she had left him. As she had done with her father when he had left her with strangers, although it had taken her a long time to learn that self-containment, shutting down on the misery of feeling hopelessly bereft and alone whenever she waved her father off in the Kombivan filled with amplifiers and instruments but not her.

She hadn't mourned when her father had died. At the funeral she had felt removed from both his life and his death, which she discovered had resulted from a heroin overdose. It was a relief to know that, in a way. Somehow it excused a lot Jayne hadn't understood, like how he could leave her as though she was excess baggage he didn't need and was only in the way.

At the time he died, she was sixteen and no longer dependent on his friends and acquaintances for anything. She had a job with a travel agent and was renting a room in a boarding house. She remembered thinking she didn't need him. She didn't need anybody.

Had she been repeating that same pattern with Dan?

Certainly she had been intent on managing without him, and she had managed. The difference was that she had missed Dan. Terribly. She hadn't missed her father.

With Dan she had learnt what it was like to be close to another person in all the wonderful ways there were to be close. Loneliness came much harder after knowing that. Yet, in the end, being with him, fulfilling the role of his wife, hadn't compensated for the unanswered needs that had become more and more pressing under the stresses of Dan's chosen way of life.

Tears welled into her eyes as those needs clawed once more through her heart and mind.

I want a home I can call my own. I want a family growing up in that home, coming back to it, knowing I'll always be there for them, and they for me. I want to be part of a community where being me means something, where I'm a participant instead of an outsider. I want to contribute something, to feel I'm not just passing through this life as a nothing person.

She was painfully aware that Dan didn't understand any of this, that his upbringing had conditioned him to the life he led. His father had been an engineer who built bridges; his mother an artist who revelled in going to the far-flung places her husband's work took them. Dan remembered his childhood as a series of marvellous adventures, the world his playground.

They were two very different people. Dan was happy making transient acquaintances with whom he became quickly involved. It made her a stranger to his life. She knew he would feel the same way if she tried to involve him in hers. He would find settling down in one place boring and too deadly dull to contemplate.

So where did that leave them?

It was the same question Jayne had asked two years ago and despaired of finding any answer that would give either of them any lasting satisfaction. All things considered, she doubted there was an answer now, especially if Dan was deeply embittered by what she had done.

Perhaps he had instinctively acted like a dog with a bone when Omar El Talik expressed his desire for her. It didn't necessarily mean he wanted her for himself.

Unless she was prepared to heat him up.

To Jayne's infinite regret, sexual compatibility was not enough on which to base a lifetime together. It simply wasn't.

She cried herself to sleep, wishing, wanting, needing ... and it didn't help at all that the man she had loved was so close ... so close and yet so far away.

She woke sluggishly the next morning. It took several moments to identify the sounds sliding into her woolly consciousness. Happy, bubbly, baby sounds. Nina's daughter. Jayne wished she had been there to help her friend in her darkest hour, although Nina's trust in Dan had not been mislaid.

She listened with sharper concentration. Not a murmur from Dan. Was he up already, armouring himself against spending the day with Dragon Lady, or still fast asleep, oblivious to the situation they were now committed to for the duration of Monty's contract with the Chinese government?

Jayne rose and dressed quietly, pulling on practical work clothes: jeans, shirt, a denim battle jacket, thick socks and heavy-duty walking shoes. She had no idea if Dan would want to visit the project site today. If so, she was dressed appropriately. If not, he'd have no cause to think she was trying to look seductive. There was nothing to gain by trying to heat Dan. Even if she succeeded, it would inevitably lead to further hurt and frustration.

Whatever he felt about her, Jayne hoped they could find some neutral ground that could make living together reasonably amicable. She didn't want to hurt him. Lashing out at each other was not going to achieve anything good. Their marriage was two years in the past. It was better for both of them if it stayed there.

She washed and did what she could to tidy her hair. She heard Huang Chunz arrive, fresh from her morning visit to the markets, and hurried out to the kitchen to inform her of the new household arrangements. Chunz had been assigned to cook and clean for Monty and Jayne. Her eyes widened in surprise and delight at hearing there was now a baby girl to care for.

As with most Chinese families in the cities, Chunz and her husband only had the one child, a boy who was now eleven and doing well at school. Chunz was immensely proud of him, although she had confided wistfully to Jayne that she would have loved to have a daughter, too. Unfortunately, in China it was irresponsible to have more than one child because of the shortage in housing and food.

'Is the baby still sleeping?' she asked.

'No, but I think Mr. Drayton is,' Jayne answered.

'She must be hungry by now. We could feed her for Mr. Drayton,' Chunz suggested eagerly.

Jayne wasn't sure that was a wise move. Dan might interpret it as interference. There had been a proud belligerence in his assertion that he took care of Baby all by himself.

On the other hand, what harm could a little baby-minding do if it allowed him to sleep on undisturbed? He must be very tired, probably jet-lagged. It was only considerate to let him have as much rest as he needed. He hadn't had any objection to Jayne holding Baby last night when he was supposedly incapacitated. What objection could he have this morning?

'I'll get her,' Jayne said decisively.

'I shall put egg in the rice. It will be good for her,' Chunz declared with a happy clap of her hands.

Knowing Dan's propensity for trying the local cuisine wherever he was, Jayne had no doubt that Baby's dietary habits were just as broad as his. She had probably been fed sheep's eyes in Morocco.

Jayne put her ear to their bedroom door, listening for any hint that Dan was awake. A few gurgles, splutters and excited little squeals indicated that Baby was in fine fettle. There was no discernible sound from Dan. Very quietly Jayne turned the handle and pushed the door open enough for her to slide into the room and unobtrusively check out the situation.

Baby had kicked off the bedclothes on her side. Her legs were up in the air and hanging suspended between her kicking feet and the clutch of her hands on its ears was a soft, toy panda bear, obviously a new and exciting acquisition. She made an absolutely gorgeous picture, snugly clothed in a red jumpsuit and playing with the black and white bear. Jayne wished she had a camera in her hands to take a snapshot.

The soft melting in her heart and the fatuous smile on her face both froze with shock as Baby caught sight of her and the bear went flying, almost smacking into Dan's nose. Jayne's feet flew across the floor and she scooped Baby up in her arms to prevent any mishap that might wake Dan. She flicked him a quick, cursory glance, saw no sign of movement, and with a sense of intense relief, hastened to the door to make a speedy exit.

'Reduced to kidnapping, Jayne?'

The husky drawl stopped her in her tracks. She spun around, excuses for her action tumbling from her mind but distracted from reaching her tongue by the sight of the bedclothes sliding off Dan's torso as he hitched himself up from the pillow.

He had a beautiful body, sleekly muscled, firmly fleshed, his olive skin sensually smooth and gleaming with health, compelling an urge to touch, to glide fingers or hands over its warm vitality. Lying naked with him had always been a tactile pleasure. It was impossible to see him like this and not remember. It had been so good...so long ago....

In sheer defence against the stirring response in her own body, Jayne stared at the St. Christopher medal dangling from the fine silver chain around his neck. His mother had given it to him when he was a boy, promising him a safe journey through life. He always wore it. There would be another journey after China, Jayne savagely reminded herself. And another. There was a long way to go before Dan reached Z and Zimbabwe.

'Answer me, Jayne,' he commanded harshly.

She dragged her gaze up to his, feeling intensely vulnerable and fighting not to show it. There was not the slightest trace of slumber in his dark eyes. They probed hers with merciless intent.

'Are you suffering a bout of frustrated maternal instinct?'

'No... I...' She recalled the anguish she had felt when she had first seen Dan with the baby. It was gone now. It had gone the moment she had learnt Baby was Nina's and Mike's daughter, that she wasn't part of Dan and some other woman. Nevertheless, it was a warning of how deeply Dan could still touch her. She had to be on her guard against that. 'I thought Baby might be hungry,' she explained defensively.

'She's had a bottle of formula. I was up earlier.'

'Oh!' It flustered Jayne that she hadn't heard him moving about the apartment. Had he looked in on her, remembering how it had once been between them? She shied away from that thought and rushed back into speech. 'You seemed to be heavily asleep. I thought you might appreciate some extra rest.'

'Considerate of you.' His mouth took on a mocking twist. 'Or was the urge to hold the baby again irresistible?'

'I told you...'

'She's so soft and warm and cuddly, so sweetly appealing. Makes your stomach curl, doesn't it?'

'I . . .' Jayne floundered. It was true, yet it was true of all baby things; kittens and puppies and chickens. It didn't mean she was broody for a baby. 'It's only natural to feel caring toward a child this young,' she said defiantly.

'Does your new career make up for the child we could have had, Jayne?' Dan asked, insidiously striking the raw feelings that had erupted through her last night. 'The baby we could have shared?'

'It's not a career,' she protested.

'You don't see yourself working your way up some business ladder, stamping your own individuality on the work you do, wielding power over others?'

She flinched at the taunting barbs. 'I never said I wanted that, Dan,' she answered with quiet dignity. 'I never did.'

'Then what's the plan, Jayne? How do you intend to establish your own identity?'

'By staying still. And putting down roots.'

He grimaced and swept her with a derisive look. 'Your credibility is in dire need of propping up. What the hell are you doing in China with Monty Castle if your heart's desire is to stay still and put down roots?'

'I needed to find my feet before choosing the best place for me to stay. And buying a home is expensive. Monty promised me a substantial bonus at the completion of this contract if I accompanied him to China.'

His eyes narrowed. 'No me, no bonus. It must have been quite a dilemma for you.'

Enough was enough. He wasn't listening to her. He just wanted to hurt. 'I don't have to account to you for what I do or don't do, Dan, except in so far as the job is concerned.'

She walked back to the bed and deposited Baby on her pillow. 'I'm sorry I intruded on your private life,' she added, quickly pulling away from the child and straightening up to meet Dan's gaze with steady, relentless determination. 'Believe me. It won't happen again.'

She was almost back at the door when he softly asked, 'Why haven't you put a divorce in process, Jayne?'

Because she hadn't wanted to think about it...about him...about the end of what had once been beautiful. She had needed more distance between them, not in place but in time before confronting the contact that would have to be made. That contact was here and now. She should take decisive action here and now. Instead she turned and challenged him.

'Why haven't you, Dan?'

A primitive flare of possession blazed into his eyes. 'You're my wife. Till death do us part.'

A man of his word, of his vows.

It shamed her.

It goaded her into bitter rebellion.

'So what's your plan, Dan? To railroad me into sharing your life again on your terms? Am I to grovel for your forgiveness first? Admit that I was wrong to give up on our marriage? Beg you to take me back?'

His jaw tightened.

Jayne knew she'd hit a nerve. She plowed on, laying her position on the line for him. 'If that's what you want, forget it. The wife you had *is* dead. I'll never be that woman again. Not for you. Not for anyone.'

She was shaking as she closed the door behind her. She heard Baby crowing, 'Da-da, Da-da . . .' She shut her eyes tight to stem a rush of tears. She couldn't let Dan get to her like this. Control . . . control was the key.

She'd let him do all the running in there, answering questions as though she was in the dock and he had the right to play the part of grand inquisitor, probing and punishing in his judgements. He wasn't God Almighty. He had flaws, too. And he could do with a strong dash of humbling.

Jayne steeled herself to set the record straight and opened the door again. Dan was propped on his side, gazing down at the child who clearly adored him. Which reminded Jayne of another issue she felt very strongly about.

He glanced up with a brooding look at Jayne and she burst into speech, giving him no chance to start on her again. 'For your information, I wasn't indulging myself in getting Baby up. Chunz, the Chinese woman who cooks and cleans for us, is out in the kitchen making a special breakfast for her. She would have loved to have a little girl of her own and she's so happy at the prospect of looking after Baby while we're here, I didn't see any harm in giving her the pleasure of doing what she wanted.'

Jayne paused for a quick breath before firing another salvo in her own defence. 'I know this doesn't fit your picture of me. I'm supposed to be too self-absorbed to care about the feelings of others or know anything about them. However, if you'd like to bring Baby out to the kitchen, you can find out for yourself that what I'm telling you is true.'

'I'll take your word for it,' he said flatly, waving her forward. 'I'm sure Baby will enjoy being fussed over and fed something different. Go ahead and carry her out to Chunz. I'll get dressed and join you in the kitchen for breakfast.'

'Right!' Jayne strode over to Baby's side of the bed again and swung the child onto her hip. 'Another thing!' she hurled at Dan.

His mouth quirked. 'I'm glad you've decided communication is better than running away.'

'Communication takes a listener as well as a talker. I don't particularly care to bash my head against a brick wall,' she retorted loftily. 'But for the sake of Nina's daughter, I will. And I'll go on bashing it until you have the decency to re-think what you've done.'

One eyebrow arched a mocking query. 'What have I done that's so reprehensible?'

'Nina would never have called her daughter Baby. Never!' Jayne declared vehemently. 'You choose a proper name for her, Dan Drayton. A name that she'll be happy with in the years to come. You owe it to Nina. You owe it to Mike. It's their child and and what you've done is turn her into a no-name person.'

The eyebrow descended into a frown.

'Think about it!' Jayne commanded. 'I want to hear your first suggestion at breakfast.'

Having thrown down her gauntlet, she marched out of the bedroom, satisfied she had done justice to herself and to Baby. Having lacked any solid sense of identity herself, no way was she going to allow Dan to burden Nina's daughter with a similar handicap. Nor was she going to let him undermine what she had achieved for herself and what she was going to achieve for herself!

He was right about one thing.

He was not going to find it comfortable living with Dragon Lady!

# CHAPTER NINE

DAN reviewed his position as he dressed. It wasn't totally bad. He was established in the same domicile as Jayne and continual propinquity could break down a lot of barriers, given time and patience. He also had answers to work on, such as they were.

At least he didn't have to take complete stabs in the dark any more. Jayne didn't want any other man...yet. The idea of sharing *his* life on *his* terms—whatever her perception of that was—aroused intensely negative feelings. Wanting a house of her own suggested a frustrated nesting instinct.

He had the outline of a picture that he could fill in as they spent more time together. For two years he had been rendered powerless to do anything about their marriage. It might not be possible to resurrect what they'd once had together, but he wasn't going to tamely accept the status quo.

The woman he had married was not dead. She was more vitally alive than he had ever seen her; challengingly alive, excitingly alive. She threw off sparks that set his body abuzz with wanting her again.

She shouldn't still have the power to do that to him, but she did. There was no denying it. She stirred him as no other woman had before, during or after their marriage. It had only taken one look at her last night for all the old feelings to rush through him again. More sharply from having gone two years without her. Every bit as sharply as when he had first seen her under a full moon in Fiji six years ago.

Having donned his heavy-duty drill clothes, he sat on the bed to pull on his socks and boots. His mind drifted back over the past six years. When had it started going wrong for her? Why?

She had been a travel agent when they'd met, as alone as he was, no ties to anyone or anything. She'd been delighted with the idea of travelling the world with him. Their honeymoon on the Northern Lights cruise from Finland had been deliriously happy, and afterward, in France, she had loved exploring Paris with him.

He sifted through the countries they had been in, trying to find signposts to her discontent. Germany... Greece... Hungary... no problems there. Iceland... such a fascinating land of natural violent wonders; volcanoes, hot springs, geysers, glaciers. Jayne had thought it chillingly barren. She'd been rather quiet, glad to leave. India...

Dan came to a mental halt.

Jayne had been disturbed by India. The poverty. Children begging in the street. The children had definitely distressed her, especially the homeless. That was when the long silences had started, the depression that somehow evolved into desperation during their stay in Iran.

Iran was hard on women. He acknowledged that. Although he didn't understand why Jayne had taken it quite so hard. She'd had Nina for company while he and Mike were working. It wasn't as though she was alone with customs that she hated. Nor was he insensitive to her feelings about it. He had crossed Iraq off his itinerary, although it wasn't as oppressive for women as Iran.

He had been quite sure Jayne would love Ireland, yet when he had told her his plan, she had stared right through him as though she hadn't heard a word, as though he wasn't even there. Then had come the bombshell that she wanted out of their marriage, and it didn't matter what he said, what he offered, it was as though she had lowered an impenetrable wall between them, shutting herself off from him.

He'd had no choice but to let her go.

Nina had said Jayne needed space in which to work out what she wanted from life. He had mentally given her three months. She'd wanted to go home to Australia. He'd seen her onto a flight to Sydney... then nothing. She might as well have disappeared off the face of the earth. The letters he'd written were returned to sender, uncollected, unanswered.

He remembered sitting with Nina through the long, painful hours before she died. 'Jayne loves you, Dan,' she had whispered close to the end. Then, with tears glistening in her eyes, 'It's so hard to give up someone you love. I'm glad I'm going to Mike, but it hurts to leave our baby.'

'She'll be safe with me, I promise, Nina,' he had assured her.

'It must have hurt Jayne terribly to leave you. I hope you find each other again, Dan. Do you think she'll mind about you having my baby?'

'No. She won't mind, Nina.'

He would have said anything to comfort her. At the time he had bitterly dismissed Nina's thoughts about Jayne. They made no sense to him. Nor did they now. People didn't leave those they loved unless they were forced to by circumstances beyond their control. That wasn't the case with Jayne.

Or was it?

*His terms...*

Had he assumed a control over her life that she had found intolerable?

He shook his head. She had said last night she hadn't thought him a tyrannical husband.

He needed more evidence of how Jayne saw things. At least he had made one right assumption. She didn't mind about him having Nina's baby. Not that she had any reason to since she didn't plan on resuming their marriage. Which made it rather odd that she was ready to fight tooth and nail to ensure he do what she considered right for the child.

He pushed himself to move, tidying the bedroom before going to the bathroom. He idly considered various names for Baby while he washed and shaved. It didn't hurt him to concede to Jayne on this point. Approval was a warm feeling. The more warm feelings he could generate between them, the closer he'd get to whatever had driven Jayne away from him.

She had Baby seated on her lap when he entered the kitchen. The mother and child picture they made knifed his heart. Why couldn't she have . . .? But he had to push his anger aside, deal with the present.

'How about Muriel?' It was his mother's name.

Jayne flashed him a wary look. 'I don't think it fits.' She nodded to a small, round Chinese woman who was bringing a steaming dish to the table. 'This is Mrs. Huang Chunz. Mr. Drayton, Chunz.'

'You have a beautiful baby, Mr. Drayton,' Chunz almost sang, her face wreathed in a huge smile.

'Thank you. And thank you for looking after us.'

'Breakfast is ready. Please sit down. I will hold the baby.' She took her from Jayne and cuddled her lovingly. 'I am happy to mind her while you work,' she offered, her eyes shiny with eager appeal.

'I thought it best we visit Monty at the hospital first thing this morning,' Jayne put in quickly, her eyes still wary as she added, 'If that's all right with you.'

'Fine.' He sat at the table opposite her and smiled at the motherly Chinese woman. 'I'm afraid Baby isn't used to being parted from me. Perhaps when she gets to know you better, she'll be happy to stay with you, Chunz.'

Her eyes dulled with disappointment. 'Any time, Mr. Drayton.'

'Chunz is very reliable,' Jayne assured him.

'I'm sure she is,' he agreed, gesturing for Jayne to serve herself first. 'So am I. Responsible, too. Nina called me a rock.'

'More like a rolling stone,' Jayne tripped out, then compressed her lips as though annoyed at herself for making the comment.

Dan reflected on it as they ate breakfast, which consisted of the inevitable rice with little cup-shaped meat dumplings wrapped in a thin, dough skin.

Jayne was intent on buying a house, staying in one place, but a house was an empty shell without the right people in it. A house didn't necessarily make a home. As for putting down roots, what value did that have? So that someone a few generations on could trace a family tree? What was a life worth unless one could pack into it every experience possible?

Was this talk of a home and putting down roots camouflage for motives Jayne didn't want to disclose? Sops to put him off? Dan was not about to be put off. If it was the last thing he did he would blow up that damned wall she'd erected between them and find out what was behind it.

'Wanda,' he said, pleased with the inspiration. 'I'll call Baby, Wanda.'

Jayne glared at him, her blue eyes intensely vivid with violent rejection. 'No, you won't. It might fit you but you can't pin that label on a child who knows nothing else.'

The vehement passion in her voice gave him further food for thought. Had Jayne's desire to settle in one place become an obsession that overrode everything else?

'Theresa,' he offered for approval. 'You admired Mother Theresa and the work she was doing in India.'

Jayne visibly shuddered. 'No.' She flicked a look at Baby. 'It's not appropriate.'

Dan ran through several other names. Jayne vetoed every one of them, saying they didn't fit. What the criteria for 'fitting' was, Dan had no idea. By the time they set off for the hospital, Baby was still Baby.

Jayne drove the truck that had been put at Monty's disposal. There was no nervous deferring of the task to him, although the hordes of cyclists that thronged the streets of Xi'an made negotiating a truck through and around them a tricky business. Jayne handled it without any evident qualms.

Dan mentally catalogued the differences he had noticed in her. She was more self-assured, very much her own person and not the least bit backward or awkward in dealing with people. He had seen her handle Lin Zhiyong and Omar El Talik with finesse last night and Huang Chunz with kindly interest this morning.

She had stood up to everything he had thrown at her, too. Her strength of mind and assertiveness had surprised him. It also forced him to re-appraise his role in their marriage. Had he been too dominant, too protective, stunting her self-growth? She was certainly a woman to be reckoned with now. There seemed nothing about her that he could take for granted.

'How about Hebe?' he tossed at her. 'Good classical name, Hebe.' He jiggled the possum bag he carried Baby in to draw her attention. 'Hebe is not so different to what you're used to, is it, sweetheart? Do you like Hebe?'

She blew him a raspberry.

Jayne laughed. Her eyes actually twinkled at him. 'I think that puts paid to Hebe.'

Dan was sharply reminded of days of love and laughter. He wanted them back. He wanted... He expelled a long breath. Jayne wasn't about to fall in with what he wanted this time around. He forced himself to relax.

'All right. I give up. You name her,' he invited.

Jayne darted an uncertain glance at him.

'I mean it,' he assured her. 'I readily confess I'm a man. I'll go with your feminine leanings and intuition. Besides, if Baby ends up hating her new name, the blame is all yours, Jayne.'

Still she hesitated. 'Have you legally adopted her, Dan?'

'Yes.'

'What's on her papers?'

'Baby Lassiter Drayton.'

She frowned. 'I guess that can be construed as not having been christened before then. Has she been baptised?'

'No.'

'Then you can put her proper names on her baptismal certificate. That will make up for any feeling of having the matter neglected before.'

*Neglected*? Dan thought that was a harsh reflection on his inclination to simply use Baby. Or was it a reflection of Jayne's feelings? He recollected her saying that her childhood wasn't worth remembering and always refused to be drawn on it. He filed that away under *questions to be answered*.

'Names?' he queried, noting her use of the plural.

'Yes. She should have two.'

'Have you decided?'

'Anya Micaela. Anya was Nina's real name. Micaela so she knows she's very much part of her father, as well. It will give her a sense of... well, family heritage. I think that's important.'

'Why?'

She threw him a startled look. 'I think most people want to belong to someone.'

'Why shouldn't she feel she belongs to me?'

A flush stained her pale cheeks. 'I only meant that adopted children want a connection to their natural parents. That's not belittling your role in her life, Dan.'

Jayne had more than belittled his role in her own life, he thought sourly. He wondered how she would react to regular incursions from him in her precious new life.

'So now we've got to get Baby baptised,' he said agreeably. 'After we've finished this project, I'll come back to Australia with you and have it done there. I think you should be godmother, Jayne. Nina would have liked that. Anya Micaela will, too. Gives her another person to belong to.'

He watched Jayne's fingers tighten around the driving wheel. The atmosphere in the cabin of the truck thickened with tension. He could feel her brain racing through the permutations, how much of a tie it would be to him, how many contacts it might entail in the future, the responsibilities she would be taking on as godmother.

Dan patiently waited for her reply, not pressing, not elaborating on the theme, allowing Jayne's caring for Nina's daughter do all the work for him. They passed through two sets of traffic lights before she came to a decision.

'I agree,' she said slowly. 'If anything happens to you, Anya will have me to come to. She can count on me always being there for her when and if she needs me.'

All Anya. No expectation that he might come along with her. He wondered why. 'That's a big commitment, Jayne,' he observed.

She grimaced. 'I know what it's like to be cut adrift. I wouldn't want Anya Micaela to ever think she had no one to go to.'

'You cut yourself adrift, Jayne,' he said harshly, unable to repress the swift rise of anger stirred by her words.

She bit her lips as hot colour burned into her cheeks again. Her chest rose and fell as she struggled to regain composure. 'I was referring to... to something else, Dan.'

'Fine! Then let me understand,' he urged tersely. 'Unlock the closets and roll out the skelctons. They might shed some light on why you saw fit to cut me adrift.'

Her eyes flashed blue fire at him. 'You've never been anything but adrift. You always will be adrift. That's your nature.'

'Is that so?'

'Yes. And I don't anticipate that anything will ever change you,' she added flatly, the fire dying as quickly as it had blazed.

The revealing little flare-up gave Dan a very clear picture. Jayne didn't believe he would stick around if he brought Baby—Anya Micaela—to visit her godmother. She felt confident there would be no more than the most fleeting connection with him. If that. It was firmly fixed in her mind that he was an inveterate wanderer, a rolling stone, incapable of tolerating a settled existence.

She probably thought her commitment was purely a safeguard, a fall-back situation for Nina's daughter should he be killed in an accident or meet some other unforeseen and premature death.

'We're here,' she announced, turning the truck through the gateway to the hospital.

Yes, we're here, Dan silently echoed, but we have a long, long way to go, Jayne Winter.

# CHAPTER TEN

As THEY walked through the hospital to Monty's ward, Jayne was uncomfortably aware that living with Dan was going to be like living on top of a volcano. No matter how much control she exerted on her responses to him, nor how tightly focused she tried to be on getting the job done for Monty, the underlying wounds from their marriage were all too ready to erupt in unpredictable and explosive bursts.

Making decisions in principle was a far cry from implementing them. Jayne tried to assure herself that as time went on, the surges of violent emotion would lessen and she and Dan would reach a truce of mutual respect that would allow some measure of peace for both of them. That sounded fine in principle, too. If only she could block out her intense awareness of him.

Just walking beside him reminded her of how well-matched they were physically. She didn't have to shorten her stride to keep abreast of him as she did with all the Chinese people working on the project. Dan was half a head taller than her but her legs were virtually the same length as his. Not nearly as powerful, though. Dan's thighs... She quickly shook her mind off that treacherous thought.

'I'd rather you didn't mention our marriage to Monty,' she said, recoiling from the idea of her boss speculating about their personal lives, past and present.

'You expect me to perpetuate your lie?' Dan mocked.

'I didn't precisely lie. I just...'

'By omission, you did.'

'What happened in my private past has nothing to do with how I do my job,' she defended hotly.

'Calling yourself Miss Winter is a deception on all the men who think you're single. Including Monty.'

'For all intents and purposes, I am single,' Jayne stressed.

Dan gave her a dark, simmering glare. 'I wouldn't broadcast that if I were you. I mightn't rescue you from the clutches of Omar El Talik again.'

'Oh, for heaven's sake!'

'Husbands do have their uses. Which you found out last night when you conveniently used our relationship to convince Lin Zhiyong everything was all right.'

Jayne didn't have any ready riposte for that.

'I haven't lived a lie, Jayne. Why should you feel the need for it?'

'I wanted to forget,' she muttered, trapped into telling the truth.

'You can put that futility in the past,' he advised with sardonic humour. 'As Anya's godmother, you'll be duty bound to remember both of us.'

Jayne sighed. He was right about it being a futility anyhow. She glanced at the sling bag within which Anya was happily bouncing against his chest. It was attached to a harness that went around Dan's neck and back, leaving his hands and arms free to do whatever he wanted. Both father and child were clearly accustomed to it and comfortable with it. No wonder their bonding was so close, Jayne thought with a discomforting, little stab of envy.

She wished she could have more to do with bringing up Nina's daughter. Little Anya was such a lovable child. Chunz was enraptured with her. It was difficult not to be. Jayne hadn't once heard her cry. As now, she was happy simply to gaze around, taking in everything with lively curiosity or fascinated interest.

Anya's life with Dan would be full of marvellous sightseeing. Would that keep her happy over the years? Would there come a time when the continuing adventure started to pall, when the shifting from place to place could not be faced anymore?

Possibly not if Anya knew nothing else, but at least she would have a godmother whose door and home was always open to her. Jayne felt good about that now, glad that Dan had suggested it.

Nina's daughter need never feel alone and abandoned with no one to care for her.

They reached the door to Monty's ward and Dan paused for Jayne to precede him. She pasted a smile on her face, determined to look on top of everything she should be on top of as Monty's personal assistant.

He was propped up in bed, looking more his old self. His face was a much better colour now, his eyes keenly alert, flicking from Jayne's smile to the face of the man following her, his mind for business not in the least impaired.

Prompted by Dan's absurd suspicion about her relationship with her boss, Jayne re-assessed him in the light of possible lover. Monty could definitely be called ruggedly handsome for a mature man in his fifties. The aging effect of his thick grey hair was minimised by tanned skin and piercing blue eyes. Physically he was on the lean side, but Jayne had thought him very fit, which had made his stroke all the more shocking.

She decided she might find him very attractive if she was fifty herself. He was a widower who frequently referred to experiences that he and his wife had shared. Jayne was positive Monty would never look to the younger generation in seeking the love and companionship he had known with his wife and he was far too wrapped up in his work to consider a wild fling.

'Well?' he asked as they lined up beside his bed. He shot a beetling frown at Dan. 'Are you satisfied?'

'Your Miss Winter and I have reached a working agreement,' Dan stated dryly.

Jayne tensed. Was Dan teasing her or did he mean to fall in with her wish to keep their marriage private?

'Told you!' Monty gruffed. 'Do you think I'd bring her on a job like this if she hadn't proved her worth? Never made a mistake in judging character yet. Picked you, didn't I?'

Jayne was mortified. Because of her, Dan might have let Monty down. *She* had been the stumbling block to a ready agreement between the two men. She silently vowed to live up to Monty's faith in her, no matter how difficult Dan made that task.

'Actually, I picked you, Monty,' Dan drawled. 'You were the best.'

Monty gave a bark of laughter. 'Until you improved on my techniques.' His blue eyes twinkled at Jayne. 'He wasn't quite so arrogant when he came to me, straight out of university with the ink still wet on his degrees. "I want to learn from you," he said.' Monty shook his head in wry reminiscence. 'Fastest darned learner I ever had.'

Jayne was stunned at hearing that Dan had once worked for Monty, virtually his professional protégé! If she'd known that, she would never have applied for the position she had, risking the possibility of being in the middle of communication between the two men. It had seemed quite safe to work for a competitor in the same field as Dan. Competitors rarely worked in the same place at the same time.

Monty grinned at her. 'Bit of a surprise, Dan turning up with a baby. He wasn't sure how you'd handle it, Jayne. I told him you could handle anything.'

'Thank you,' she said thinly, inwardly railing at the coincidence that had involved her with Dan once more.

So far he hadn't revealed their marriage to Monty. Pride probably had more to do with it than her appeal. It hardly made Dan look good to lay claim to a relationship she had rejected. She hoped he would let sleeping dogs lie.

'Well, now that this is settled, I have another proposition to put to you, Dan,' Monty said with an abrupt return to serious business.

'Should I leave the two of you alone?' Jayne quickly interposed.

'No. It'll affect you, Jayne. You might as well know what's in the wind.'

She didn't like the sound of that, although it was only to be expected that Monty would have to re-think the immediate future. Even though there were good signs for a recovery from his stroke, it would take time.

'As you know, arrangements have been made for me to fly home. I'll be in rehabilitation therapy for quite a while. Which leaves Castle Construction without a working head.' He gave Jayne a rueful smile. 'I know you'd see that any orders I gave were carried out, and you'd keep a meticulous check on everything, but you can't take my place, Jayne.'

'No one could,' she said, impulsively reaching out to touch his arm in a gesture of respect and affection.

'Not true.' His gaze shifted to Dan. 'This stroke is a warning for me to slow down. Take life a lot easier. My daughters and their husbands wouldn't have a clue how to carry on what I've built up, Dan, and it'll crumble without me.'

'Monty, if you're proposing what I think you're proposing, I'm not for hire,' Dan warned. 'This China project is a one-off thing. Okay?'

Jayne could have told Monty that. Apart from being very much his own man, no one was ever going to tie Dan down to one place.

'I don't have a son,' Monty went on. 'If I could have chosen one, it would be you, Dan.'

'Well, that's mighty complimentary, and I appreciate the regard it implies, but...'

'I'm offering you a partnership, Dan, and all you have to bring into it is your expertise.'

Jayne's breath caught in her throat. The company assets alone ran into millions. The huge earth-moving equipment, the yards, the construction side of the business...

'I'm not a desk jockey, Monty.'

Jayne shook her head. Stupid to think he might be influenced by a massive increase in worldly goods. Nothing was going to divert Dan from his chosen path. Not love, nor money, nor even a baby. Didn't she know that?

'You can hire those,' Monty said with a dismissive wave of his good hand. 'It's the head behind the hiring that I want. Damn it, Dan! I don't want to see my life's work sold off or going down the drain. You've got the right feel for the jobs that should be taken. You don't blunder. Everything you've done is cost-effective and profitable. Do you think I haven't watched your one-man career?'

'Monty, you haven't thought this through,' Dan stated matter-of-factly. 'Your family won't like it, giving away half of the company.'

'It's mine to give,' Monty argued, his face setting into belligerent lines.

'I understand that the stroke has shaken you up, but you might recover much faster than you anticipate,' Dan pointed out. 'This offer is premature, Monty.'

And futile, Jayne thought, impatient with Dan's careful reasoning. Postponing the issue was tantamount to encouraging Monty to think about it further. It was unfair of Dan to give the slightest thread of hope when he knew he was never going to accept. Jayne sliced him a reproving look. He caught it and raised his eyebrows.

'You have a problem, Miss Winter?'

Trust Dan to put her on the spot! 'It seems to me that if the answer is no, the answer is no,' she stated unequivocally.

'How black and white you are, Miss Winter!' he said icily.

'Jayne, this isn't your business,' Monty warned.

'It is if she doesn't like the idea of me becoming her boss,' Dan corrected him. 'Do you have a problem with that, Miss Winter?'

'No. None whatsoever. I can work for any boss,' she replied with all the confidence of knowing Dan would not stay around to be her boss for long.

'You'd keep on in your position if it meant assisting me instead of Monty?' Dan persisted.

'Why shouldn't she?' Monty asked.

'I really don't see that happening beyond this job in China, Mr. Drayton,' Jayne said bluntly, feeling that this kind of game-playing was out of order and out of taste. 'Australia doesn't fit between M and Z.'

'Neither does China,' he reminded her, his eyes narrowing on the sparks of resentment blazing from hers.

'What are you talking about...M and Z?' Monty demanded irritably.

'Mozambique and Zimbabwe,' Dan answered,

turning a smile to Monty. 'A travel plan I had before you called me here.'

'You'll have your choice of where you want to go if you take the partnership. It's up to you how much travelling you do or don't do. Reputation has to be maintained,' Monty pointed out.

'Monty, you're not yet finished,' Dan said kindly. 'Don't make decisions now.'

At last a bit of good advice, Jayne thought, although Dan should, in all integrity, put the matter beyond question.

'I won't change my mind, Dan. Give it your serious consideration. I mean it.'

Jayne gave Dan another hard, challenging look. Finish it! she mentally commanded him. Don't hold out false hope!

He appeared to be weighing the proposition. He raised a sardonic eyebrow at her, his eyes flashing with a derisive glitter at her obvious concern. However, when he addressed Monty again it was with deference and deadly seriousness.

'It's a handsome proposition, Monty, but it would mean a change in life-style for me and Baby Anya.'

Finally the truth!

'Given that I make the change, like you, I wouldn't want to lose what I build up,' he went on with barely a pause. 'Or see it wasted. To be blunt, Monty, in the event of your death, your family could demand a sell-up and I might not have the capital to buy them out. As generous as your offer is, I'd need more to tempt me.'

Jayne could hardly believe her ears. Dan was still holding out a carrot.

Monty was urged on. 'Spell it out, Dan.'

'Even while you're still alive and kicking, Monty, I'd want control. I'm not in the habit of answering to anyone. What I decide is what's done. If you want me to head the company, I need to have the power to head it.'

'Fair enough!' Monty agreed. 'Put it in hard terms.'

'Complete ownership of fifty-one percent of the voting shares.'

'Done!'

Monty held out his hand to shake on the deal. Jayne stared down at it, incredulous that this was actually happening. It couldn't. Dan wouldn't take that hand. If he did...

She waited in painful suspense, feeling as though she was poised on the rim of a volcano. She'd want to throw herself in if Dan accepted. It would mean she had misjudged him, ruined both their lives on a terribly mistaken notion that he would never be happy tied to one place for the rest of his life. Her perception of him would be blown to smithereens.

But then, he was an explosives expert.

Yet he could not have foreseen this situation, nor been prepared for it.

His hand did not reach out to clasp Monty's.

'No. You think about it, Monty,' he said softly, caringly. 'It's a big step to take and I don't want to be accused of taking advantage of you in a weak moment. I'll fly on to Australia when we've finished up here. We'll talk again then.'

The painful activity in Jayne's mind flattened out and the cramp in her heart eased. Dan was humouring Monty, wanting to remove any burden of worry about the future from the older man's mind until the present health crisis passed. He had no intention of actually settling.

Monty chuckled, dropped his hand to the bed-cover and relaxed back against the pillows. 'I've got you. You've always been a man of your word, Dan.'

'One of my many failings,' Dan said dryly.

Monty smiled up at her. 'Look after him, Jayne. He's my man.'

'I'll do my best, Monty,' she assured him, not prepared to disturb his peace of mind.

'Now go off and blow up mountains,' he bade them cheerfully. 'I don't want to see either of you again until this job in China is done and you report back to me in Sydney.'

They left the ward. As they made their way out of the hospital, Jayne reflected that Dan would have no trouble keeping his word to Monty. He planned to fly to Australia anyway to have Anya baptised with Jayne as her godmother. He wouldn't have to go far out of his way to have a chat with Monty.

'That was very tactful of you,' she remarked, then couldn't help adding, 'Though somewhat deceptive.'

He gave her an ironic look. 'You think I was being deceptive?'

She hesitated. 'Weren't you?'

'I think I'd call it a wait-and-see situation,' he drawled.

She frowned, hating the feeling of uncertainty. 'Do you mean...if Monty still offers you fifty-one percent after a cooling-off period, you'd actually accept it?'

They reached the truck and he turned to face her, his eyes burning with relentless purpose. 'You know, Jayne, when I saw Mount Everest for the first time, what came into my mind was how would I go about shifting it.'

'What does that have to do with anything?' she asked in bewilderment.

'For some reason I find unfathomable, you've built a mountain between us. One way or another, I'm going to shift that mountain. I don't care what it takes. I'll find out what's needed to blow it apart. And every other mountain you try to put between us, I'll blow apart. I'll reduce it all to rubble so I have a clear vista of who and what you are and who and what you want to be.'

'Why?' she cried. His determination was frightening in its single-mindedness. He wasn't even looking at, let alone considering long-term consequences. 'Why is it so essential for you to control things?'

His gaze raked her from head to foot, searing in its intensity. 'You might be Dragon Lady to everybody else, but not to me. To me you are the woman who was and should still be my wife, and I'll fight for that with any means that comes within my orbit.'

Jayne's heart kicked into overdrive. He wanted her back with him. He wanted their marriage resumed. He wanted ... A danger klaxon shrieked through her mind. He might want too much, as he had before!

'So, to get a controlling interest in me, you'd even take up Monty's partnership offer. Is that your intention?' she asked, to determine how far he would go for her.

'This isn't a power game, Jayne. Not to me. For a wife who wanted me ... for a wife who wanted to have my children—' his mouth curved sensually and his voice was a skin-tingling caress '—for her I would consider doing many things.'

'Even settle in one place?'

'Surely between people of goodwill, compromises can be found.'

She recollected Monty's assurance that Dan could choose wherever he wanted to travel. How much would he really consider her needs when it came down to living with them?

Jayne scooped in a deep breath and very slowly released it. 'We have work to do,' she said bruskly, and, steeling herself against the emotional tug on her heart and the sexual magnetism that was pulling on her bones, she forced her legs to stride around to the driver's side of the truck and climb into the cabin.

If they were to make love and have a baby, it would be in *her* time, on *her* terms, she dictated to herself. Nevertheless she couldn't deny the heady mixture of hope and excitement leaping through her mind. This wasn't a case of her following Dan. He was actively chasing her. But she wasn't going to get caught until she was absolutely sure of what getting caught would mean for her.

# CHAPTER ELEVEN

JAYNE tried to keep level-headed as she worked closely with Dan. They did not take days off. The schedule was tight. The project had to be completed on time. They were constantly on the move, constantly together. The strong physical attraction between them was also ever constant, evoking a high-tension awareness that played havoc with Jayne's concentration on her job as Dan's assistant.

More insidious were the reminders of all the character traits she had loved in Dan, as well as other aspects of his personality she had not really been privy to before. During the four years as his wife, she had never seen him at work, never experienced what it was like to be with him as he went about his business. It was a revelation.

He didn't just walk in and assume authority as he had every right to do as an acknowledged world expert in his field. He talked to the Chinese engineers, one by one, respectfully drawing from them their opinions and ideas on the mudflow problem, picking their brains of all local knowledge, showing keen interest in every bit of information he drew from them.

They liked him for it. He made them feel important. He injected the sense of everyone being a vital part of a team. In return, they quite naturally perceived him as a leader they instinctively trusted to put it all together and get it right for them. He earned their goodwill, their ready cooperation, as well as Jayne's admiration and a much deeper appreciation of why Monty wanted Dan to head his company. It was not only Dan's expertise in explosives. It was his expertise in leadership.

Then there was the way he treated her when he reviewed Monty's files on the project. He complimented her on her orderly and efficient presentation of notes and maps, listened attentively when she filled him in on other points of progress to date, was unreservedly vocal in his appreciation of her general comprehension of what was required in her job as his—Monty's—personal assistant.

There was one short conversation Jayne could not help hugging to her heart.

'I can see why Monty values you so highly,' Dan said with genuine spontaneity, then followed the observation with a rueful smile and the admission, 'I'm sorry for pigeon-holing you as simply my wife, Jayne. If I'd realised your potential for such meticulous organisation with this kind of work, we could have shared so much more.'

His recognition of her worth as an assistant made her glow with pleasure. But was it a promise for the future, or merely an acknowledgement of a past mistake?

'Travel agents have to check everything and get the scheduling right,' she remarked, more as a statement of fact than a criticism of his oversight. 'You never gave the impression you needed any help. I would have offered.'

He mused on that for several moments before answering, 'Heritage, I guess. My dad never asked nor expected my mother to help with his work. He was happy with her being happy doing her own thing.'

'Then perhaps your ideal wife should be an artist who can fulfil her talent in any environment without the need for others to contribute anything.'

'No.' He grinned, sending electric charges through her nervous system. 'I don't want to feel shut out of any part of my wife's life. I like this better.'

For now... or for always?

It was a question that endlessly teased Jayne's mind.

She was his wife... if she wanted to be... and each night she found it harder and harder to shut him out of her bedroom. Not that he made any overt sexual advance on her but he made no secret of what he desired. It was in his eyes all the time, the tempting invitation, the seductive sizzle of his intimate knowledge of her, the unremitting challenge to take up what he offered, to risk the outcome and the consequences.

Jayne was acutely aware he was leaving the decision to her. He wanted her to show she wanted him, show it unstintingly, unreservedly, to choose him of her own free will, for better or for worse, to wash away the negative residue from having left him with a positive flow of faith and love and enduring commitment.

Sometimes she wished he would make it easy for her by just sweeping her into his arms and obliterating all her doubts and fears in a searing outpouring of passion. Yet she knew that was pure and desperate escapism, not an answer to her sense of insecurity about what a future with Dan might mean in terms of real togetherness.

She watched him with Anya, who went everywhere with him. Not even the tricky operation of setting the explosives in the mountains deterred Dan from taking Anya along. For the most part, his role in this work was supervisory, although he stepped in to make corrections whenever the Chinese engineers didn't quite follow his instructions to the letter.

He talked to the baby as though she took in and understood every word he said. Somehow the communication seemed to work because Anya always responded to him with grave, innocent trust or a burst of baby chatter that Dan interpreted with paternal indulgence.

Why did communication get so difficult as life patterns took on more individual twists and turns?

The wonderful bond Dan and Anya shared was a further torment to Jayne. She couldn't imagine a better father for the children she wanted herself. Eventually. When the circumstances were right.

Was it possible to strike a happy balance between her needs and Dan's? Or at least a workable balance? How far would he compromise on a style of life he enjoyed?

A wait-and-see situation. That's what he had said. No assurances. No guarantees. Wait and see... The words haunted her. It was the kind of thing her father had said when she asked him where he was taking her this time... taking her only to desert her again.

The nights were longer and lonelier than ever before, her sleeping pattern more and more shallow and restless. She awoke with a thumping headache from some formless nightmare one night and couldn't stand the silent, claustrophobic darkness of her bedroom for another minute.

She leapt out of bed, switched on the light, quickly wrapped herself in a housecoat to ward off the sudden chill of the predawn hour, then hurried out to the kitchen to take some painkillers and make herself a cup of tea. She needed something warm inside her, warm and calming.

She was seated at the table, hunched over a
steaming teacup, feeling despairingly bereft of
all human comfort when she heard footsteps
padding softly down the hallway toward the
kitchen. There was nowhere for her to hide. She
watched helplessly as Dan filled the doorway, the
only exit back to the privacy of her bedroom.

She knew she looked pale and bedraggled. She
felt a total mess, mentally, emotionally and physically. She couldn't bring herself to meet his eyes.
She stared fixedly at the deep V of tanned chest
left naked by his loosely tied bathrobe. A black
bathrobe. Was it the same one she'd given him
for his birthday? Would he have kept it, worn it
for over two years? It seemed to have the greyish
tinge of well-washed age.

'Are you all right, Jayne?'

The soft, caring words curled into her mind
and wound their way down to her heart,
squeezing it unmercifully. She dragged her gaze
up to his, helplessly imploring answers she knew
he wouldn't—possibly couldn't—give.

'Jayne?'

She saw the concern in his eyes flicker uncer-
tainly then recede, swallowed by a dark turbulence that enveloped her with urgent tentacles
of need and want. His hand lifted, reaching out.
He took a step forward.

'No,' she cried, a desperate croak of denial.

He checked himself.

'I'm not all right.' The words spilled from a deep chasm of emptiness inside her. 'I've never been all right. For a while, with you, I thought I had everything I'd ever wanted. You gave me so much I had craved, Dan. And I'm sorry... I'm sorry it wasn't enough. I'm sorry I couldn't take it anymore. I can't...I can't...'

Her throat convulsed. Tears welled into her eyes. Impossible to stem the flow. She struggled to find Dragon Lady, to make her emerge with the inner fire of purpose that had sustained her for so long, but the fire was drowned in a tidal wave of tears pressing to get out, uncontrollable. And then it didn't matter anymore. Nothing mattered. The grief for what had never been had broken out of its locked container, swamping everything else.

# CHAPTER TWELVE

DAN was momentarily paralysed with uncertainty. He'd thought she was about to give in. He'd set out to win her back, charm her, convince her, seduce her if necessary. But this heart-wrenching torment...

Tears... A woman's weapon... Yet Jayne had never used it. In all the time he had known her she hadn't once wept for or over anything. Not even when she had left him. She had turned inward, presenting a stone face that denied him entry to her thoughts and feelings. The frustration of it had been maddening. For her to break down like this... God! What had he done to her in his determined drive to make her his wife again?

Disappointment and grief twisted through him. Hadn't two years given him the message she didn't want him in her life? What right did he have to crash his way into a world she was trying to shape for herself?

Wanting the satisfaction of proving she had been wrong to end their marriage had fired him along this track. Certainly there was pride involved, though it went much deeper than that.

He had wanted, still wanted, the love that had once been theirs.

How to comfort her? Would she accept comfort from him? Couldn't a husband—even an ex-husband—be a friend who cared about her? More than cared, he mocked himself, but concern for her was uppermost as he moved to the table and slowly lowered himself into the chair opposite hers.

She had propped an elbow on the table, her hand covering her eyes. Her other hand lay limply beside the teacup. He reached across and gently stroked her fingers.

'It's no use,' she choked out. 'I can't, Dan.'

'I'm not pushing anything, Jayne,' he soothed, encouraged that she didn't reject the light skin contact. 'I'm sorry, too. I didn't mean to hurt you.'

'Not your fault.'

He frowned, not understanding. Streamlets of tears were tracking down her cheeks, dripping from her chin. The sheer abandonment of any attempt to wipe away or mop up the steady spill screwed up Dan's stomach. He couldn't stand it. He curled his hand around hers, pressing with what he hoped felt like warm reassurance as he urged her to accept the only ready offer he could make.

'Jayne, honey, I haven't got a handkerchief on me, but this old towelling robe can soak up a fair lot of moisture. You gave it to me yourself, so we've already had some sharing time with it. You could treat it as an old friend to lean on. No more than that, I promise you.'

The response shattered any reasoned thinking. Jayne burst into more anguished sobbing. Before Dan could give any consideration to what he was doing, he was on his feet and pulling Jayne out of her hunch and up from her chair, wrapping his arms securely around her as she sagged against him.

'You just let go now, love. Let the pain out. You're safe with me,' he heard himself murmur huskily, his lips sweeping over the tangled silk of her hair, his nostrils sucking in the scent of it, arousing an almost sick yearning for all he had just forbidden himself. Yet the helpless yielding of her body to his strength, to his support, brought a surge of tenderness, a fierce desire to protect, that took away the initial sting of his need for her.

He rubbed her back with the same soothing gentle action he used on Baby Anya when she had a bit of colic. He laid his cheek on her hair, wanting to cocoon her in the comfort of other human touch so she didn't feel alone. He thought over what she'd said, trying to make sense of it, wanting to fix whatever was so shatteringly wrong for her.

'What can't you take anymore, Jayne?' he asked softly.

Her body shook with another convulsive burst of weeping.

'Is it me?' he rasped in anguish. 'Do you want me to go? Get out of your life?'

'No...no...'

The tightness in his chest eased as he breathed again. Her face burrowed into the thick cloth covering his shoulder. She snuffled like a wounded child in need of succour. His arms tightened around her, yearning to impart a healing love.

'Tell me, Jayne,' he pleaded. 'Let me help.'

'I...don't...know...if you can. It's... not...fair.' She hiccupped, struggling for some control. She sounded deathly tired. Exhausted. 'You're...you, Dan.'

'And you are you. I want to know, to understand. Please...if it doesn't hurt too much?'

She snuffled some more, took deep breaths, laid her head limply on his shoulder. 'All my life...endless moving...the people...a passing parade of strangers. No time to fit in and belong. Like a shadow of a person. No substance. I didn't count. I didn't mean anything to anyone. Until I met you.'

'You mean more to me than I can tell you, Jayne,' he assured her with deep fervour. 'Believe it. It's true.'

'Oh, Dan!' It was a long, tremulous sigh of longing. 'I loved you so much. You made me feel important.'

'You were. You are.'

'But you wanted to move on...and on. And I lost myself again. It all became unreal. As though I was a marionette being pulled along by your strings. And I can't face that feeling again. I'm not like your mother. Nor mine,' she added dully.

'Yours?' This was new territory for him. He felt compelled to explore it as far as he could. Later he could think about what she was telling him, what it meant in terms of the love and life he wanted to have with her.

'She went everywhere with my father. I think she kept track of things for the band. It was their life.'

He vaguely recollected Jayne telling him her father had been a musician. Her mother had probably had the organizational skills Jayne had inherited.

'I don't think she minded where they went as long as it was together. The band was like a family to both of them.'

'Not to you?'

'I guess...in an offhand kind of way. They found places for me to live...people who'd take me in for a while...after my mother died.'

'How old were you then, Jayne?'

'Seven.'

And here she was, twenty years later, still without what she had needed all her life. A secure home base. People that she knew, who knew her, down the continuity of years of knowing. Acceptance, approval, appreciation for all that she was and could be. Substance. Roots.

He closed his eyes and barely stifled a groan as the signposts she'd given him flashed through his mind with poignant power.

The need to establish her own identity.

Satisfaction in using the skills she knew she had.

Pride, self-respect . . . not a nothing person nor a second-class citizen without a voice of her own.

A home for Anya Micaela to come to if she ever needed it, wanted it.

And the self-absorption he had accused her of . . . she didn't know any other way to survive except to turn in on the inner strength that she had silently depended on with no other supportive constant in her life.

The insights came so strongly, not only filling in the picture he had wanted but colouring it so vividly he could feel himself recoiling from the emotional neglect and the intense personal isolation that were the sum of her experience . . . except for what she had known with him . . . for a while.

'Dan . . .'

'Mmmh?'

'Thanks for holding me up and giving me your robe to cry on.'

'The least I could do,' he said with sad irony.

'I'm all washed out, Dan.'

She sounded it, drained and infinitely weary.
'I'll walk you to your bed. You might fall or
stumble.'

'I'll manage.'

'Don't argue. I'm your boss and I need you
on your feet tomorrow. Okay?'

She sighed and sagged her surrender to his
management. He bent and scooped her off her
feet. She needed to be carried. He wanted to carry
her, wanted to hug her close, protect her, cuddle
her.

She didn't resist. She hung her arms around
his neck and nestled her head against his cheek
like a forlorn little child. It moved Dan
deeply... the implicit trust in him, the instinctive
faith that he would look after her.

He wished he had looked after her with far
more care and attention and knowledge when
they were married, instead of assuming he did
his fair share of giving in the husband role, being
the provider, the planner, the decision-maker, the
achiever for both of them.

It hadn't entered his head that what he was
doing was literally pulling her along with him,
wanting her to ride beside him on his merry-go-
round, blindly dismissing the obvious indica-
tions that she was finding it difficult to cope with
the changes he rang whenever it suited him.

He found himself in Jayne's bedroom, beside
her bed, with no memory of having negotiated
the passage here. He didn't want to put her down.

She was clinging to him. He turned and sat on the bed, holding her on his lap, reluctant to part from her. She needed him. To leave her alone would be wrong. She wasn't all right and she'd feel even less all right if he left her alone, prey to more torment in the isolation of darkness.

He cleared his throat. 'Jayne, honey...' The endearment was probably a mistake. She might think... Damnation! How could he put it?

'I'm going to stay with you and hold you until you're sound asleep,' he said in a decisive rush. 'There's nothing for you to worry about. I won't take advantage of being close to you. I don't want you lying here alone, thinking bad thoughts. It wasn't wrong for you to cry and tell me things. It was good. And if you want to tell me more, I'm here to listen.'

He hoped that was enough reassurance.

She stirred, turning her face into his throat. Her breath was a warm caress on his skin, arousing memories, needs that he couldn't let himself dwell on.

'Is it asking too much...?' she began hesitantly.

'Anything you want,' he promised gruffly.

'Would you lie with me spoon-fashion, Dan? That always made me feel at peace somehow. I've missed it so.'

'Me, too. They were the best times.'

'Yes.' It was a long, dragged out sigh of contentment, and the soft fullness of her breasts swelled and eased more closely against his chest.

Dan felt himself stir, the muscles around his loins tightening. How the hell was he going to stop an erection, lying next to her like that? Did she remember it was how they had lain together *after* they had made love, when every desire had been satisfied and the sweet languor of absolute satiation had drifted into the peace of utter fulfilment?

He tried to block it out of his mind as he busied himself removing her housecoat and putting her to bed. He couldn't resist stroking her glorious hair out on the pillow and pressing a soft kiss on her forehead.

'Won't be a moment,' he murmured.

He walked swiftly to the light switch and turned it off. The darkness was a relief. He didn't want her to see the need, the temptation in his eyes. It was *her* need that had to be satisfied, and he wasn't going to let her down. He had promised her.

He moved back to the bed, paused, his whole body tingling with anticipation. It wouldn't feel the same if he kept his bathrobe on. He wasn't completely naked underneath it. He'd taken to wearing boxer shorts to bed since Baby Anya had become part of his life. It wasn't too much of a liberty to have his chest and arms bare. Jayne was wearing a cotton nightie.

He cast off the bathrobe and climbed into bed beside her. She was already turned on her side. He slid an arm under her neck, cushioning her head against his shoulder. Slowly, and applying the utmost control over wayward impulses, he fitted his body to the soft curve of hers, gliding his other arm around her waist to snuggle her closer to him while carefully avoiding contact with her breasts. Then he forced himself to relax.

She wriggled her bottom more comfortably, more intimately against his groin, then sighed as though the feel of him was heaven.

To Dan, the feel of her was both heaven and hell.

Two years...

Was there only to be this at the end of it?

## CHAPTER THIRTEEN

THE stroke of gentle fingers softly raking her hair away from her face brought Jayne out of her deep slumber. She opened her eyes to bright morning light and to Dan sitting on the edge of her bed, freshly shaved, fully dressed, his dark gaze keenly watchful.

'Do you want to sleep on or do you want to come to work with me?' he asked.

She frowned at her bedside clock, realising it must be later than her usual rising time.

'I switched off the alarm,' Dan explained. 'Chunz has packed a breakfast for you. You can eat it in the truck on the way. All you have to do is wash and dress. Or stay in bed if you don't feel up to it.'

'No. I'm fine.'

She sat bolt upright to prove it. His hand trailed away. She caught it, her heart pumping a self-conscious flush over her skin as she remembered the intimate confidences of last night and his compassionate responses.

'Dan . . .' She quickly searched his eyes, feeling intensely vulnerable. 'Thank you for...for being so generous.'

He shook his head as he rose to his feet. He looked down at the hand still holding his and slowly rubbed his thumb over the knuckle where she had once worn his rings. 'Penance for my sins, Jayne,' he said sardonically.

'Please don't think like that. I can't blame you for the way I am,' she said earnestly, squeezing his hand in a flood of warm feeling for the wonderful person he was.

His gaze lifted to hers, darkly passionate. 'I blame myself for not seeing it.'

'You don't have to,' she cried, hating the sense of having burdened him with guilt. She scrambled to her knees in urgent appeal, inadvertently pinning the thin cotton of her nightie. The neckline pulled down, cutting across the swell of her breasts. 'Oh, damn!' she muttered, struggling to free the tangle of cloth around her legs.

Before she could loosen the garment, Dan caught her around the waist and swung her up from the bed and onto her feet, facing him. 'There's one thing I need to know,' he said, his eyes hotly purposeful.

'What?' she asked breathlessly, the warm grasp of his hands making her feel acutely fragile as far as any defences went.

'Whether the fire is still there for me?'

There was no mistaking his intention to kiss her. He gave her fair warning, bending his head slowly, his gaze dropping from hers, fastening on her mouth. Confusion reigned in Jayne's mind, caution warring against the impulse to give, as Dan had given to her last night.

His lips tingled over hers, sending disruptive electric impulses through her brain. Jayne was literally incapable of making any move. It was as though all her life-force was focused on the exquisite sensations streaming from his mouth to hers. She'd been starved of any kissing for so long and Dan did it beautifully with soft, lingering pressures, tantalising flicks of his tongue, seductive little nibbles. She couldn't resist tasting him again.

She slipped her tongue into his mouth, searching for and stroking the sensitive spots she knew were there. He responded with a burst of passionate action, sweeping her body against his in a crushing embrace, kissing her with a hunger so intense he shook with it. It stirred an answering hunger in her, a wild craving for all the unfed love of two long years.

Her arms wound around his neck, fingers weaving through the dark springy curls to close around his head and hold him to her. They kissed and kissed again and it wasn't enough. The heat of desire ran helter-skelter through her body, every pulse point throbbing with urgent excitement. She swayed, instinctively seeking the friction that would satisfy the heightened sensitivity of her barely clad flesh.

His hands slid down the curve of her spine and closed around the soft mounds of her buttocks, intensely possessive as he lifted them, straining her closer to the thrusting hardness of his aroused manhood. A groan tore from his throat as his mouth broke from hers, leaving Jayne dizzily intoxicated with wanting him.

He arched his neck as though desperate to gulp in air. She felt his body ripple with tensing muscles. Then he lowered his head and his eyes were a dark blaze of searing purpose.

'Say you want me, Jayne,' he commanded.

How could she deny what was so starkly evident—her lips kiss-swollen from her need of him, the sweet agony of desire throbbing between them?

'I want you, Dan,' she whispered, her eyes the open windows to a truth that was impossible to hide.

His chest expanded and the breath left his lungs and hissed through his teeth. He relaxed his grip on her, lifting a hand to her face, one finger slowly tracing the contours of her mouth. His eyes softened to dark velvet.

'There's no time now for all that I want to feel with you, Jayne. Promise me that tonight will be for us.'

Time...of course! The schedule was set. It had to be kept. She struggled to get her brain in sensible order. A horde of primitive instincts screamed to fling caution to the winds.

There had only ever been Dan for her. What harm could it do to renew the intimacy they had known, even if it was only for a while? When it came time to go their separate ways...she shied away from that thought, her mind and heart intent on seizing the here and now.

'Yes. Tonight,' she promised him.

Another deep breath, sifting through a dazzling smile. 'I'll go and check on Anya. I left her with Chunz.' He gently released her and stepped away. 'You won't take long to get ready?'

'Ten minutes.'

He nodded and left her, striding swiftly to the door. A very special man. More special than she had known before. If they could forge a new, deeper dimension of togetherness, working beside each other... Jayne's mind whirled with feverish hope as she raced to the wardrobe for her clothes.

*Wait and see...*

It didn't mean nothing could be changed during the *waiting*. When it came to the *seeing*, maybe they would both come to a deeper appreciation of how their lives might fit together. *If* Dan was really prepared to take up Monty's offer. *If* the offer remained open. If, if, if.... Maybe she was fooling herself, but suddenly it seemed utterly essential not to shut the door on possibilities.

The minutes flew by. When Jayne arrived in the kitchen, she was greeted by a beaming Chunz rocking Anya in her arms. 'I am to mind the baby today. She will be very happy with me. I promise Mr. Drayton to take good care of her.'

Jayne couldn't help smiling at the Chinese woman's delight. 'I'm sure you will, Chunz,' she said warmly, the warmth extending to Dan for giving Chunz the pleasure of having the little girl to indulge with her motherly loving.

'Ready?' he asked.

'Yes.'

He scooped a packet off the table, blew a kiss to Anya, who smacked her lips in response, and gestured for Jayne to lead the way. 'I'll drive while you eat,' he said, passing the packet to her as they headed for the door.

Jayne had the feeling of being cosseted, as well as having matters taken out of her hands. Once she was settled in the passenger seat of the truck, with Dan supposedly concentrating on the road, she had the definite sense of some shift having occurred in the atmosphere. The cabin seemed charged with energy, as though a host of positrons was zinging around.

Her gaze was drawn to Dan.

He caught her seraching look and grinned, emanating a sparkling vitality that made her heart dance. 'Don't even consider having second thoughts,' he warned. 'I'm a man with a mission.'

'To blow up mountains?' She laughed, suddenly bubbling with happiness.

'And capture the Dragon Lady,' he affirmed.

'How will you keep her captive?'

He sliced her a sharply knowing look. 'I never would. I have no intention of doing so.'

'Then it's merely a feat to be accomplished?' she queried.

He shook his head. 'The man who captures Dragon Lady can only win time with her, time she is willing to give. That is his reward.'

'He wouldn't take her away from her lair?'

'Only if she wanted to spread her wings and fly with him. Dragon Lady must always be free to be where she wants to be or she will lose her fire.'

She couldn't ask for anything fairer than that from Dan. Whether such an arrangement would satisfy them in practice, she didn't know, but nothing was going to stop her from trying it. The understanding it conveyed, the respect and caring, filled her soul with joy.

She opened the packet he had handed her and found it contained the fried dough sticks that Chunz called *youzhagui*, meaning 'fried devils'.

'I have learned some things about China, Dan,' she said impulsively, remembering his scorn at her ignorance about the Chang Er legend. 'They have wonderful stories behind the names they give their food.'

She waved one of the dough sticks at him as she recited what Chunz had told her. 'Once upon a time a general was so infuriated by his enemies, he made effigies of them in dough, which he fried and ate. That's why these are called fried devils.'

He laughed, his eyes twinkling warm pleasure. 'Reading a Chinese menu is sometimes like reading a fairy tale. Monk Jumps Over The Wall is my favourite.'

'How does that go?'

'A meditating monk was distracted by a delicious smell wafting from the other side of a wall. It was dried seafood stewing in a pot. In the end, he couldn't bear it any longer and jumped over the wall to ask for a bowl.'

'I like the very fanciful ones like Red-Beaked Green Parrots On White Marble. You know what that is?'

'No.'

She wrinkled her nose. 'Spinach served with boiled bean curd.'

'How about Ants Crawling Up A Tree?' he retaliated.

The light-hearted swapping of food information formed a relaxed and companionable conversation as Jayne ate her breakfast. By that time, they were well on the way to the site of the new city of Denjing where all construction had ceased because of the threat of a destructive mudflow. Jayne's thoughts turned to the serious work ahead of them. Only then did she realise what Anya would be missing by not being with them today.

'Aren't we scheduled to detonate?' she asked.

'Yes, we are. Lin Zhiyong will have the honour of pressing the button.'

'Then why did you leave Anya with Chunz? You said she liked big booms.'

'She won't know she's missing them, Jayne.'

'Is it particularly dangerous today? Do you expect something to go wrong?' she asked anxiously.

'No. Not with the explosions.'

'Then why leave her behind?'

He hesitated, then gave her a crooked smile. 'I thought something might go wrong with you. I didn't want to have to think of Anya, too. Not today.'

'Oh!'

Jayne turned away, flushing at the realisation that Dan must feel very uncertain of his ground with her. Did she seem unstable to him? Did he feel he had to be on his toes to block any retreat from her decision to give him tonight?

'I promised you, Dan,' she said quietly.

There was a short, nerve-twanging silence before he replied, just as quietly, 'Promises can be given in good faith, Jayne. Sometimes things happen. Circumstances change. What at first seems right turns out to be wrong. And promises get dropped.'

Jayne's flush grew more painful.

Dan had always been a man of his word.

It was she who had broken her promises in walking away from their marriage. He might now understand why she had done so, but the bottom line fact was, she had not stayed true to the commitment she had given him.

*Till death do us part.*

She shivered, suddenly feeling very unworthy of the man beside her. He had every reason not to trust her word. But she would change that tonight. More words were meaningless. She had to show him with action. Very loving, very positive action.

She looked out at the mountains that were fast approaching. The skyline around the new city of Denjing would be different after today. She hoped a lot of things would be different after today.

There were five huge peaks ahead of them, thrust out of the crust of the earth at strange angles and reaching up to the heavens in a cluster that had moved Monty to christen them 'The Hand of God'. That name would have no meaning once Dan's explosives took their toll. It had to be done for the greater good of the people of China. Yet...

Jayne had an eerie sense of premonition.

Please...she found herself praying. Please don't let anything go wrong before tonight.

# CHAPTER FOURTEEN

THERE were various factors contributing to the mudflow problem. First, China was a predominantly mountainous country with proportionately little fertile farmland to feed its ever-burgeoning population. In the rainy season, huge amounts of silt and grit washed down from the highlands into the rivers.

In the lower reaches, the mud inevitably built up, causing the riverbed to rise. To prevent the flooding of rich farmlands, a system of constant dyke-building was used to contain the river.

This could only be considered a stopgap measure as the dykes had already been raised to a dangerous height. Scientists and engineers agreed that the only long-term answer to this problem was to keep the mud out of the river.

Above the site of Denjing, engineers had been damming the gullies and pumping river water up to wash the soil from the mountains into the gullies to create new farmland which would feed the new city. Unfortunately the tree-felling and the dislodging of vegetation that had accompanied this exercise had destabilised the whole area.

Rapid erosion had taken place on the steep slopes during the last rainy season, resulting in a mudflow that warned of the disaster to come if the weather brought heavy precipitation in short periods.

Mudflows could rush down a mountainside at speeds as great as a hundred kilometres per hour, moving boulders as large as houses. There was only one solution to saving the city of Denjing. The mountains had to be moved.

The explosives had been set. By the end of the day, the gorges and chasms that gave dangerous passage to the city site would be filled with such massive amounts of rubble that the course of any mudflow would never find its way to Denjing. Indeed, the series of detonations should create a terraced effect so that the different levels could trap rainfall, helping the process of turning the landfill into productive farms.

That was the theory, anyway. Monty had believed it would work. Dan was confident of making it work. He had examined the terrain, supervised the setting of the explosives, and apparently anticipated everything going to plan.

Although Jayne was not in any way responsible for the outcome, she couldn't help feeling nervous about it. She dearly wanted everything to turn out right; for Monty, for Dan, for the Chinese people whose livelihoods were involved.

Once they arrived at Denjing, she and Dan were transported by army helicopter to the plateau where the detonations would be set off. It provided the best vantage point for watching what happened. Theirs was not the only helicopter in action. A number of them were lined up on the plateau.

A large party of government officials from Beijing had come to witness the proceedings. Lin Zhiyong was playing host to them. The importance of this occasion to him was enormous. If the project was a success, it would be a huge increase of face for him personally. If it was a failure, he would be very much out of countenance.

Jayne was the only woman present. The visitors eyed her with circumspect interest. She was introduced as Miss Winter, personal assistant to Monty Castle and Dan Drayton, but she had little doubt she was being summed up as Dragon Lady. Several times she was called upon to explain the scale models that demonstrated the proposed effect of the explosives, as though she was as much an expert as Dan was.

Finally, Lin Zhiyong gave a formal speech along predictable lines until he came to the end of it. 'I will now call upon Miss Winter to press the detonating button,' he said, startling her by passing over the honour.

She shot a questioning look at Dan, who whispered, 'Sidestepping responsibility.'

'Miss Winter has overseen this project from its beginning,' Lin Zhiyong continued. 'She is a lady who makes things happen.'

The wily, old diplomat gave her a respectful bow and gestured her forward to perform the final act. Jayne knew she couldn't hesitate, not as Dragon Lady nor as Dan's wife. Her heart skipped around her chest as she stepped up to the dais to an accompanying round of polite applause.

She smiled at Lin Zhiyong, swept the smile around the crowd of observers to Dan, turned it up several megawatts for him in order to demonstrate her absolute confidence in his expertise, then turned to perform what had to be done. She gave everyone time to don the earmuffs provided, then used her thumb to press firmly.

There was an eerie silence.

They saw the mountains erupt before the vibrations and sound hit them. It was a big boom, a very big boom that went on and on while the earth beneath them shook. Time seemed to be unnaturally extended. Clouds of dust billowed up, obscuring their vision of the awesome changes taking place, but the rumble continued unabated for what felt like hours.

Eventually the noise subsided and the dust began to settle. Earmuffs were removed. Excited chatter broke out in Chinese. Jayne had no idea what was being said. Dan moved to her side, slid an arm around her waist and hugged her close. It felt good. Especially when he smiled at her.

'You did it, Dragon Lady,' he crooned softly. 'Breathed fire into the mountains and knocked them flat.'

She smiled back at him. 'You can't give me credit for that, Dan.'

'You heard Lin Zhiyong. You make things happen.'

'No. You do.'

'Let's compromise on being partners.'

'I'd like that,' she said simply, hoping he was referring to the future.

The warmth in his eyes made her glow inside. Surely it was not merely for this moment of success.

If success it was.

Lin Zhiyong called them to join him in a helicopter ride over the blasted area. Only a bird's-eye view would confirm the results of the operation to everyone's satisfaction. Once again, earmuffs were donned so conversation was impossible, but Jayne was sweetly aware of a sense of intimate togetherness as she sat beside Dan in the army helicopter.

Nothing could now go wrong with today, she thought. Unless the helicopter crashed. In which case, she would go down with Dan and they would never be separated again. But she would much prefer to make love with him first, to know again the passionate enslavement of her senses with his, to feel the intense closeness that melded them into one being.

Jayne was soaring on even more of a high when a comprehensive sweep over the area revealed a landscape that was virtually an exact replica of the *after* model. Her vivid blue eyes sparkled at Dan and her breath caught in her throat at the raw desire that blazed back at her.

It was part of sharing something special like this, her mind reasoned, a grand and awesome triumph. But her body rejoiced on a purely instinctive level, wanting what he wanted, revelling in riotous anticipation of sharing everything with him in a much more elemental fashion.

They landed back at project headquarters where they had left the truck. Lin Zhiyong abandoned his usual enigmatic manner and pumped Dan's hand with enthusiastic congratulations, his Buddhalike face beaming with an irrepressible smile. He thanked Jayne profusely, remarking she was a lady who would be greatly honoured by the new citizens of Denjing.

It was obligatory to stay for the celebratory refreshments that followed. They had to politely listen through several speeches. Lin Zhiyong, in his benevolence, invited them to a banquet at his home, a ten-course duck dinner, he boasted.

Luckily, he named the following evening for the occasion. Jayne was well aware of how long and very filling Chinese banquets were. Anything that might interfere with or postpone her night with Dan was unwelcome.

At last all their professional obligations were discharged and she and Dan could retire gracefully from the gathering. The spring of urgency was in their step, excitement, a heady intoxicant. They were brilliantly alive, the barriers were down, and they could make things happen together.

As they approached the truck, a black, official-looking car pulled up beside it. Come to collect one of the important guests, Jayne thought idly, until the door opened and out stepped a man in Arab dress.

'Uh-oh!' Dan breathed, and stopped walking.

Jayne instantly halted beside him, her heart fluttering with the intuitive knowledge that here was trouble. She was relieved to see it was not Omar El Talik who approached them, but the man was undoubtedly an emissary from the arrogant sheikh. It was too coincidental that he arrive at the completion of Dan's job in China for him to be anything else.

Dan's hand gripped Jayne's hard, his fingers interlacing with hers, revealing his inner tension . . . or an urgency that nothing or no one interrupt their time together.

'What is it?' he asked curtly, impatiently, when the man blocked their path.

The Arab bowed. 'Greetings from His Excellency, Sheikh Omar El Talik.'

'I have no further business with the sheikh,' Dan stated coldly.

The Arab regarded Dan with black, reptilian eyes. 'His Excellency believes you will change your mind, Mr. Drayton,' he stated with a confidence that sent a chill down Jayne's spine.

'No,' Dan replied succinctly.

'Your obligations here have been fulfilled,' the man argued.

'Irrelevant. I do not wish to work for your sheikh. The matter is closed.'

'His Excellency has taken steps to persuade you, Mr. Drayton.'

Dan's fingers tightened possessively, protectively. 'There is nothing that can persuade me.'

The black, snaky eyes pinned Jayne's. 'I'm sure your heart is softer, Miss Winter.'

'Not where His Excellency is concerned, no,' Jayne said firmly.

'But where your child is concerned? Your baby daughter?'

'Anya?' Fear struck her heart. Dan had warned that Omar El Talik was not above kidnapping to get his own way! 'What have you done with her?' she cried.

'Do not be alarmed, Miss Winter. She is in safe-keeping. In fact, your Chinese woman would not be parted from her.'

'Chunz? You've taken Chunz, too?'

'It seemed . . . practical.'

Jayne's mind whirled with horror. The poor little Chinese woman would feel so desperately anxious, so responsible, having been trusted to look after the baby. Yet if there was any fault, it lay with Jayne herself and Dan's concern over her emotional state. In the normal course of events, Dan would not have left Anya with Chunz today. She would be here with them, safe from the clutches of Omar El Talik and his henchmen.

'What's the deal?' Dan demanded, his voice steely, revealing no emotion whatsoever.

'His Excellency would like both you and Miss Winter to join him in his private jet. You are invited to fly with him in comfort to Morocco.'

Jayne shuddered. They wouldn't have a chance to get away once they were in the sheikh's native country! All this pseudo politeness would disappear and they'd be treated like the prisoners they were with Baby Anya held as hostage for their absolute co-operation in whatever Omar El Talik wanted of them. Jayne had no illusions about what he wanted of her.

'I see,' Dan said slowly. 'What time does he intend to lift off from Beijing?'

'As soon as we arrive, Mr. Drayton. If you'll accompany me to my car, we'll be on our way.'

'Tell Omar El Talik that my wife and I will be his guests on board his private jet.'

The shock of Dan's swift decision, without any consultation with her, threw Jayne into a further spin. They couldn't tamely give in to such crimi-

nal blackmail. There had to be some way to
rescue Anya and Chunz. They needed some de-
laying tactic, time to think, to plan.

'However, we are anxious to see to the
wellbeing of our child as soon as possible,' Dan
continued bitingly. 'We will not tolerate a slow
journey by car. We shall fly to the airport by
helicopter.'

Jayne's frantic thoughts slid to a halt. It was
reassuring to hear Dan spelling out *his* terms. She
should have known better than to think he would
surrender to any other man's terms.

The Arab's face tightened threateningly. 'You
will come with me.'

'A deal is a deal, old son,' Dan said
contemptuously. 'Don't overplay your hand.
Omar is getting what he wants.'

The snake eyes narrowed. 'Do not overplay
yours, Mr. Drayton. We have the child. We also
have diplomatic immunity. If anything of an unusual nature occurs, we will fly off immediately.'

Jayne immediately started worrying again.
They couldn't storm the sheikh's plane if he had
diplomatic immunity. How were they going to get
Anya and Chunz away from them?

'Understood,' Dan clipped out.

The Arab gave him a long, black, venomous
stare, then swung around in a swish of robes and
headed back to his car.

Dan didn't move.

Jayne couldn't. She was paralysed with the sickening sense of helplessness that came to any parents with the knowledge that their child has been taken. Not that she was Anya's mother, but she had taken Nina's daughter to her heart and there was no doubting Dan's fatherly love for the little girl.

She'd been worrying about something going wrong between her and Dan before tonight. In her own selfish need, she had not once given a thought to something going wrong with Anya. It felt like a punishment, one she would have to live with for a very long time.

'What can we do?' she cried in sheer anguish as the black car moved off.

Dan turned to her, his face grim and determined, fire and fury in his eyes. 'I'm going to blow that bastard's wings off!'

# CHAPTER FIFTEEN

JAYNE felt the blood drain from her face as the vision of engines bursting into fireballs filled her mind. 'You can't blow off his wings, Dan,' she gasped.

'Watch me!'

'It's too dangerous!'

'So, I take out insurance. Come on. There's no time to waste.'

He pulled her after him as he strode back toward the conference room at project headquarters, irreversible purpose in every step. Shattered by what seemed total recklessness to her, Jayne barely kept up with him.

'We need to think about this,' she pleaded in protest.

'It's perfectly clear-cut to me.'

'Anya is on that plane. And Chunz,' she argued.

'There's one thing you're overlooking, Jayne,' he answered matter-of-factly.

'What?'

'How you deal with people like Omar El Talik. If they deliver a threat, you deliver a bigger one. Then you trade.'

A threat. Jayne's mind whirled. It was just a threat. He didn't really mean to blow the wings off. And he was right about her not having much expertise in dealing with people. His skills in that area were far broader and far superior.

'You think it will work?' she asked, feeling the need for reassurance.

'The truly dangerous people are those that don't care what happens to them, fanatics who are ready to die for what they believe is a greater goal. Omar values his skin too much to risk it. That's his weakness.'

'But he'll have to believe you can do what you threaten.'

'He'll believe it. I make a very good fanatic when it comes to defending my wife and child from egomaniacs who can't take no for an answer. If he pushes it, I'll give him a demonstration,' Dan said grimly.

'You can't!' Jayne cried in horror.

'We've got all I need here. Plastic explosives...'

He meant it! The shock of his clearly stated intentions put a wobble in Jayne's legs. Dan was an expert, she frantically reminded herself. He should know what he could and couldn't do with safety. But, dear heaven! Was he in his right mind?

She followed willy-nilly as he pushed his way through the milling crowd in the conference room and claimed Lin Zhiyong's attention. He briefed the Chinese official on the situation and appealed for help.

'What do you have in mind?' Lin Zhiyong asked cautiously.

Dan told him. To Jayne's amazement, Lin Zhiyong didn't so much as lift an eyebrow at Dan's plan. He listened attentively, nodded sagely, then remarked, 'The immediate objective is to block the flight path so it is impossible for Omar El Talik to take off.'

'Yes,' Dan agreed.

Lin Zhiyong turned to one of his important guests from Beijing and a rapid conversation in Chinese ensued. Telephone calls were made. Lin Zhiyong received a nod and explained to Dan and Jayne in English.

'Within minutes the plane will be surrounded by army vehicles. The sheikh has a Chinese citizen on board. It is not permitted that he take a Chinese citizen out of our country without any proper procedure. That is the reason for this action if it is questioned in diplomatic circles.'

'What if he lets Chunz go?' Jayne asked anxiously.

'Sheikh Omar El Talik will not be given the reason for the blockade. Even if he works it out for himself, we will, of course, have to question Chunz, and make a formal protest to the embassy. It will all take whatever time you require, Mr. Drayton.'

'Thank you. The helicopter to transport Miss Winter and myself?'

'No problem. I shall accompany you. So will Guo Ziyun. He will co-ordinate what you require at the airport.'

'We'll need fire trucks on standby,' Dan pressed.

'They will be there. A show of strength may be necessary. That is understood. It is good that you are an American citizen, Mr. Drayton.'

'So is our baby,' Dan informed him.

Lin Zhiyong's eyes brightened. 'That is even better. We wish to establish more goodwill with your country.'

Jayne barely stopped herself from rolling her eyes. Never mind that Dan's plan would put their lives in terrifying jeopardy! The Chinese officials were viewing it as a possibly fruitful public relations exercise! Was anyone besides herself pausing to think about how badly wrong it might all turn out?

Dan left to collect his weapons of war from the supplies in storage. Jayne was asked to dictate a report which both she and Dan would sign as evidence of the situation, their plan to correct it, and the cooperation requested of and given by the Chinese government. It was proof to produce in the event of their deaths, she thought fatalistically, having moved beyond protesting anything.

The helicopter flight to Beijing could not have evoked a greater contrast in mood to the earlier flight she had shared with Dan. Far from generating any elation or sense of excited anticipation in Jayne, it became a nightmare of ever-growing tension as they flew closer and closer to a confrontation that would require nerves of steel.

Jayne could only pray that Dan was right in his reading of Omar El Talik's character. She well remembered the man's arrogance and pride. Would such a man accept the humiliation of defeat and surrender his hostage without trying to cause some damage in retaliation? Jayne found it difficult to imagine that some price wouldn't be paid for Anya's and Chunz's freedom.

The pilot took them over the blockaded private jet before landing. The sheikh had to know he was trapped on the ground by now and was probably in a rage about it. If he touched one hair on Anya's head . . . Jayne felt a surge of rage herself, obliterating the underlying fears, and realised, in some measure, what Dan was feeling.

This was the child he had promised Nina to keep safe, a child he had come to love very deeply, who was now inextricably part of his life. He would fight for her with every weapon at his disposal.

His daughter.

His wife.

He was fighting for her, too. Had been fighting for her since the festival of the full moon. The sudden insight slammed into Jayne's mind. His tenacity, his tenderness, his...love.

It had to be love. It was more than desire, more than possessiveness, far more than pride. He cared about her feelings and her needs. He truly did. She was precious to him and he would fight to protect her. Fight like a fanatic!

Jayne was abuzz with these thoughts as they were quickly ushered from the helicopter to a set of offices within the airport terminal. Backed by Lin Zhiyong's and Guo Ziyun's authority, Dan immediately set about organising his plan of action; his best line of approach to the plane to set the explosives, the cover he required, the fire truck teams at emergency readiness. She watched him give orders like the leader of men he was and felt an intense pride in him...her man...her husband.

Then he looked straight at Jayne and there was something in his eyes that turned her heart over; a yearning, a promise unfulfilled, an ironic hail and farewell. He turned to Lin Zhiyong and said, 'Whatever happens, Miss Winter is to remain safely with you. Agreed?'

'No!' Jayne broke in vehemently. 'I'll stay out of the way while you set the explosives but you're not going onto that plane without me, Dan.'

He sliced her a steely look. 'You've proved you have a life apart from me, Jayne. Anya hasn't.'

'I don't want a life apart from you,' she declared, her vivid blue eyes ablaze with that conviction. 'Not anymore, Dan. We go together. Partners.'

A muscle in his cheek contracted. 'You could be a liability.'

'I could be necessary. What if Chunz is hurt? You'll need me to hold Anya,' she argued fiercely.

'If something happens to me, you'll be here for Anya. It's what you promised, Jayne,' he replied, unmoved from his decision.

'If you don't come back for me after you've set the explosives, I'll walk out to that plane myself. I won't have you making my decisions for me, Dan. Have you forgotten that Omar El Talik wants me?'

He frowned.

'If something happens to you, he'll use Anya to get to me anyway.'

'You don't go,' he said stonily. 'No matter what eventuates, you don't go.'

He turned back to Lin Zhiyong to make this clearly understood. Before he could say a word, Jayne swung on the old Chinese official whose respect she had earned.

'I will not be stopped.' She flung up her chin in proud defiance of his authority and anyone else's. Her bright red hair shimmered in a flying cascade of tossed curls. She breathed in. Her eyes stabbed blue fire. 'I will not be stopped by anyone.'

Dragon Lady had spoken!

The words rang around the room, imprinting themselves on everyone's mind. They all stared at her. Jayne maintained her pose of absolute personal autonomy, daring anyone to try to shake it.

Lin Zhiyong cleared his throat. 'I believe Miss Winter will be of help to you, Mr. Drayton. I have learnt not to underestimate her powers.'

Dan reappraised her determination and gave her a wry little smile as he acceded to her will. 'So be it. You'll wait here until everything is ready?'

'Until then,' she agreed. 'Please be careful.'

He nodded and left.

Lin Zhiyong moved to her side. 'You would like to watch, Miss Winter?'

'Yes.'

He took her to the air-controllers' room from where they could view what was happening around the sheikh's private jet. She watched Dan and one of the Chinese engineers approach the plane from the tail end and use the undercarriage to hide their activities. Dan set the explosives and timing devices close to the tips of each wing, his assistant handing him what he needed when he needed it. Jayne breathed a sigh of intense relief when the task was safely completed and the men retreated from the plane.

'He is a man worthy of you, Miss Winter,' Lin Zhiyong said quietly. 'A man of fire and action.'

'Yes,' she answered simply, although she doubted, at that moment, she was worthy of Dan. 'He is a man of his word,' she added, knowing how deeply true that was.

He returned for her as he said he would.

Together they walked out openly to the private Lear jet of Omar El Talik.

Partners in life. Partners in death, if necessary.

# CHAPTER SIXTEEN

Two Arabs with AK-3 assault rifles flanked the door as Jayne and Dan entered the plane. They looked tense, angry and trigger-happy. The blockade had clearly had an unnerving effect.

The interior of the plane had all the luxurious comfort that could be packed into a small living room, but not one of its occupants was comfortable. Sheikh Omar El Talik was on his feet, ranting at another gunman who was seated opposite Chunz. The motherly little Chinese woman was cowering in the chair opposite, clutching Anya protectively to her chest. For the first time Jayne heard Anya wailing in distress.

Chunz looked at Dan in desperate appeal. 'I tried . . .'

A bullying tirade from her guard reduced her to quivering silence.

'Tell your man to lay off!' Dan commanded.

'Tell the army trucks to pull away!' Omar El Talik snapped back, clearly infuriated and frustrated by the restriction to *his* freedom of movement.

'That's entirely up to you, Omar,' Dan drawled, as though he was perfectly relaxed about the situation.

Jayne appreciated that it was an attempt to defuse the explosive tension and immediately took her cue from him, determined to appear calm and collected despite the knots in her stomach.

'The Chinese government doesn't take kindly to having one of their citizens abducted and flown out of the country,' Dan explained, maintaining his pose of casual ease. 'Let Chunz go and they might let you go,' he advised in a tone of reasonable logic.

Omar glared long and hard at him, then took the bait, swinging to Chunz and waving an imperious arm. 'Put the child down and leave! You are no longer of any use.'

Chunz rose tremulously to her feet and bravely defied him. 'I will not let you have the baby. She is entrusted to me.'

Omar swore viciously.

Jayne swiftly stepped forward, holding out her arms. 'Give Anya to me, Chunz,' she commanded, then, more softly, 'You have more than fulfilled your responsibility as a caring mother. Dan and I are here now. There is no need for you to stay.'

And every need for her to go, Jayne thought, willing Chunz to obey without any further protest or hesitation. Omar El Talik was in a volatile mood. The situation had escalated out of his control and Jayne suspected fear was feeding his anger, making him more aggressive and more dangerous. He might have second thoughts about following Dan's advice.

Chunz's eyes filled with tears as she looked to Dan. 'I am sorry, Mr. Drayton.'

'You carry no blame, Chunz,' he assured her kindly. 'You must now leave Anya with us and go in peace.'

She bowed her head to his authority and passed Anya over to Jayne. One less victim if it came to the worst, Jayne thought gratefully. Dan gently squeezed Chunz's shoulder in a salute to her courage and steered her toward the door.

The sheikh signalled to his men to let her make an unhindered exit. The thunk of the door closing behind her was a welcome sound to Jayne. Chunz was a total innocent. At least she didn't have to suffer any more from these thugs.

Omar El Talik glowered balefully at Jayne and Dan, then posted himself at one of the aircraft's windows to watch the outcome of releasing the Chinese woman.

Jayne tried to soothe Anya's distress but it was Dan who stopped the wailing. He inserted his index finger into one tightly closed little fist and stroked his thumb over Anya's soft, baby skin. 'It's okay, sweetheart,' he crooned. 'Daddy's here.'

It was as good as magic. Anya unscrewed her eyes, turned the noise down to a hiccup, looked at Dan, then broke into her version of a conversation to which Dan answered by nodding his understanding and giving his interpretive replies.

'Yes, a lot of wrong things happened.

'No, you shouldn't have been subjected to such upsetting events.

'Daddy's come to look after things now.

'You belong to Jayne, too.

'We're going to make everything right again, aren't we, Jayne?'

'Yes,' she agreed huskily.

Anya looked up at her, back to Dan, then with a contented little sigh, nestled her head on Jayne's shoulder, and was at peace with her world.

Love and trust, Jayne thought. That was the magic formula. Why hadn't she trusted Dan to understand when she had become lost in their marriage? She had judged for him, denying him the chance to break the self-imposed barrier of all the insecurities she had nursed in the dark places of her soul. She had resented the decisions he had made for her, yet it was she who had made the worst decision of all, forcing Dan to live with it without knowing why.

Strange that she should see it so clearly now, at this moment of crisis when their lives were most threatened. Love was not enough. Perhaps there was no real love without trust. That was why their sexual compatability had failed to influence her in the end. It took more to hold a marriage together.

Love and trust...no secrets. It had to be love and trust, unreserved, unguarded, given and taken with absolute faith in each other. Nothing, ever, could go badly wrong between them if they shared that. Only outside forces could part them, and then only physically. The bond could not be sundered.

She looked at Sheikh Omar El Talik, tensely watching what was happening outside. His force was that of a marauder, wanting to take, regardless of cost, but what she and Dan shared was invincible if they made it so. It was up to them, and especially her. Given another chance, she would not hold anything back from Dan. He would know where he stood with her, now and always.

The sheikh swung around, his eyes burning with hostility. 'The woman was met and led away. There is no movement from the trucks.'

'Perhaps Chunz was not enough,' Dan suggested dryly.

'What game do you think you're playing?' Omar demanded, waving wildly at Jayne and Anya. 'I have all the cards here.'

'Not so, old son. I have one or two up my sleeve.' He gestured Jayne toward the armchair Chunz had vacated. 'Might as well wait in comfort, sweetheart. Anya does get rather heavy after a while with no other support but your arms.'

'Wait for what?' Omar snapped, enraged further by Dan's calm, indulgent manner.

Dan waited for Jayne to sit down before ostentatiously checking his watch. 'If you look out the window, Omar, you should see fire trucks moving toward your right wing.'

He looked, then snarled at Dan. 'What is the meaning of this?'

Dan shrugged. 'They'll try to contain the damage when your right wing blows up. That should be in about thirty minutes if I set the timing device correctly. Hard to calculate the result. I daresay you're all tanked up for the flight out of here.'

The sheikh's dark skin turned sallow. The fear was uppermost now, sapping his resolution to continue a venture that had suddenly turned into a suicide mission. 'You're bluffing,' he blustered.

Dan shook his head. 'I never bluff about my business.'

'You wouldn't put the lives of your wife and child at risk.'

It was a potent argument. Jayne could see Omar El Talik puffing himself up to defy Dan's claim.

'It wasn't his decision,' she spoke up proudly. 'I told Dan I'd rather die than become your woman.'

A little bit of fabrication hardly mattered at this point, Jayne reasoned. She wanted Dan to know she was one hundred percent behind him.

Her declaration drew a glazed glare from the sheikh. Jayne's vivid blue eyes blazed their contempt for him.

'So whatever your scheme is, Your Excellency, it's not going to work,' she stated unequivocally.

'Are you mad?' Omar squawked.

'Tut-tut,' Dan chided. 'I'll smash your face in if you insult my wife.' His eyes glinted admiration for her show of support and fearlessness.

'I'll have you shot!' the sheikh retaliated. 'I'll have you all shot. The baby first.'

'Go right ahead, Your Excellency,' Jayne invited scornfully. 'It will save us the pain of burning to death. If the right wing doesn't get us, the left one will.' She looked appealingly at Dan and reinforced the threat. 'You did put more powerful explosives on the left wing, didn't you, darling?'

'Sure did, Jayne, honey,' he affirmed. 'I always do what you ask me to. It's timed to blow in about fifty minutes.' He gave the sheikh a quirky smile. 'The Chinese don't call her Dragon Lady for nothing. You shouldn't have fooled with her, Omar.'

There was a ring of pride in his voice that curled around Jayne's heart and claimed her as his woman and partner. It was a wonderful feeling. It diminished the sense of danger, removing it to a far place that didn't matter anymore. She and Dan were united as one.

Omar El Talik looked from one to the other, clearly of the opinion they had both taken leave of their senses. Jayne hoped he was recollecting that he had been unable to sway her from her set course with his offers of designer clothes and jewels and the jet-set life. The realisation that he was dealing with fanatics of the worst kind sank in. Beads of perspiration broke out on his forehead and upper lip.

He pointed a shaking finger at Dan. 'You can stop this!'

Dan checked his watch again in a desultory fashion. 'To tell you the truth, Omar, I'm not sure I can dismantle the bomb on the right wing before it blows. If you want out, you'd better get moving. I'd advise leaving the guns here. Waving them around in front of all the soldiers out there might not be diplomatic.'

'I and my men have immunity.'

'Not everyone might understand that. Assault rifles tend to make people nervous,' Dan advised gravely. 'If you want safe escort to your embassy, I'd look mighty peaceable if I were you.'

The sheikh from Morocco seethed with impotence. He really had no choice if he wanted to save his skin, but he hated losing to Dan, especially in front of his men. Finally he cracked and barked a string of orders in Arabic.

There was a great deal of hurried movement. The pilot and a steward came from the direction of the cockpit. Guns were laid down. With his men lined up weaponless beside the door, Omar

El Talik stabbed one last bitter glance at Jayne and made his exit with an imperious stride. He was quickly followed by all his attendants.

Dan inhaled a long, deep breath and slowly expelled it. He grinned at Jayne, his eyes dancing with elation and happiness. He clicked his heels and swept her a gallant bow. 'My lady, may I be permitted to escort you and our precious bundle to safe ground?'

Jayne laughed, bubbling over with relief and delight at the successful outcome of their daring. She rose from the chair, holding Anya securely in her arms. 'Sir Knight,' she said loftily, 'I'd be very grateful if you would. Post haste!'

Once they were out on the tarmac, Dan relieved Jayne of their precious bundle, hoisting Anya up against his shoulder and securing her there with one arm. Then he reached for Jayne's hand and interlaced his fingers with hers, sending electric tingles right up her arm.

Ahead of them, Omar El Talik and his men were being marched by a military escort to two black cars. There was a great roar of engines as the army trucks began a retreat from their blockades. A Jeep pulled up beside Dan and Jayne, providing them with a lift out of the danger area. They climbed in.

'Could the bombs be dismantled in time?' Jayne asked curiously.

'No problem,' Dan answered with carefree confidence.

'But you haven't told anyone that,' Jayne surmised.

'No one can mess with my family without paying a price. I said I was going to blow the bastard's wings off and that's precisely what's going to happen.'

A man of his word.

Jayne was perfectly content to leave it uncontested.

'Besides...' Dan grinned at her and jiggled Anya to draw her attention '...Baby missed out on the big booms today, didn't you, cuddlepie?'

'Boom-boom,' Anya chorused happily.

'That's absolutely right. Daddy's got two booms coming up for you.'

Jayne laughed, feeling incredibly exhilarated. Maybe it was a highly charged flow of adrenaline coursing through her now that all danger was past, but echoing through her mind was the intense emphasis Dan had given to the words, *my family*.

'The explosions are going to leave an awful mess for people to clean up,' she observed ruefully.

'No one's going to mind, Jayne. It'll make great television.'

'There aren't any TV cameras here.'

'Yes, there are. This whole exercise will be beamed around the world. Lin Zhiyong is dead set on it.'

'Because you and Anya are American citizens?'

'Partly. It also makes good propaganda for how the Chinese deal with a hostage situation.'

'But it was your plan.'

'You made it stick, Jayne.' His eyes locked onto hers, dark and turbulent with deep emotion. 'Your fire. Your determination. Without you...' He swallowed, shook his head, his eyes more eloquent in expression than any words.

She squeezed his hand. 'You'll never be without me again, Dan. Not unless you want to be.'

She meant it, every word of it. And now it was said, openly, honestly, from the deepest reaches of her heart and mind and soul.

No secrets.

Where and how the future would be shaped was now up to Dan.

# CHAPTER SEVENTEEN

DAN didn't want any negative vibrations intruding on this, his first night with Jayne for over two years. The apartment in Xi'an would undoubtedly evoke a sense of violation since Anya and Chunz had been taken there. Apart from which, he couldn't bear the loss of time in travelling.

He had a private word with Lin Zhiyong, who was only too happy to arrange for a suite to be immediately available for them in The Palace, a hotel that advertised itself as an oasis in the heart of Beijing. It combined the grandeur of the past with the luxuries of the present. Luxuries were definitely on Dan's agenda tonight.

From the moment they arrived at the hotel they were given celebrity treatment; flowers everywhere, complimentary fruit and champagne, the hotel staff offering instant attention and swift service for anything they required. The best of everything. And so it should be for Jayne, Dan thought, wanting her to feel cherished and admired and respected for the marvellous woman she was.

A cot was produced for Anya, with toys to entertain her. A new set of baby clothes and diapers were brought. She was bathed, fed, pampered, and finally put to bed. Tonight she would sleep by herself. As dearly as he loved his adopted daughter, Dan wanted, needed, to spend this night exclusively with Jayne.

It had been a long, eventful, fateful day. If Jayne was too exhausted... well, he could wait. He would make himself wait. She deserved the best from him. He'd give her anything she wanted. He still felt awed, humbled by the person she had become without him.

Yet there was no doubting she wanted him back as her husband. The decisive commitment to him had blazed in her eyes. She hadn't asked for promises or guarantees. She had simply and unequivocally placed herself in his keeping, trusting him with her life, her dreams, her love.

A fierce determination burned in his mind and pumped through his heart. He would not let her down. He would never again take a decision without her participation and approval. Partners in everything.

'I desperately need a long, hot shower,' she said, sighing her relief when they at last had complete privacy. She flopped into a chair and pulled off her shoes and socks.

He moved before he realised he was moving, drawn irresistibly to touch, to express the feelings she stirred in him. 'You must be tired. Let me help.'

He lifted her to her feet. She came fluidly, unresistingly, a weary little smile suggesting she was grateful for his offer. She stood still as his hands slid the denim battle jacket from her shoulders. As brave as any soldier could be, he thought, yet her shoulders were softly fleshed, womanly. He eased the sleeves down her arms. The jacket dropped to the floor. Neither bent to pick it up.

'We used to shower together,' she said huskily.

Her eyes were dark blue pools, fathoms deep, inviting him to drown in their luminescent warmth. 'I'll wash you,' he murmured, his fingers working quickly to unbutton her shirt.

Her fine, silky skin pulsated under his touch, her breasts lifting with tantalising fullness as she took a deep breath. He hurried to remove her shirt, her bra, dying for the exquisite pleasure of seeing, feeling, the lush femininity of her body unveiled.

She was breathtakingly beautiful. Always had been. Always would be to him. Her nipples stood out enticingly, the aureoles dark, extended, revealing her excitement, her desire to be loved. He didn't have to wait. She wanted him.

The painful control he had exerted over his need for her burst under the rampant rush of desire that shot through his body like red-hot needles. His loins throbbed with an urgency he could barely contain. The constriction of his clothes grew acute. His fingers trembled as he unfastened her jeans and tugged them down her long, lissom legs; satin thighs, the sensual curve of knees and calves, the narrow delicacy of her feet.

He was so aroused, he was tearing off his shirt as he stood again, wanting to press his flesh against her. 'Jayne...' he breathed hoarsely, pleading for her understanding. He meant to be patient. He would be. He wanted her to feel more loved than she'd ever felt before. It was how he felt. But his body had a life of its own.

'It's been so long,' she whispered, her hands reaching up, sliding yearningly over his chest, making his heart hammer with an intensity that flooded him with tingling heat.

Boots, socks, pants; he flung them away from him. He swept her into his embrace, trapping her body against his. A shuddering reaction of sheer pleasure rippled through him as her soft, voluptuous nakedness yielded to his tension-hard flesh.

'Jayne...' It was a groan of gut-wrenching relief. She was his again. The words from the marriage service, *to have and to hold*, pounded through his mind. 'I want you to know there wasn't anyone else for me.'

'Nor for me,' she said, her lips feathering his throat.

'No other woman could ever be to me what you are. And now you're so much more. Like a rosebud that has burst into magnificent bloom.

And I swear to you I'll nurture this bloom until the day I die.'

She wound her arms around his neck and leaned back, her lovely, vivid face glowing with pleasure. 'I believe you, Dan.' Her voice was a seductive purr, her mouth barely parted, her lips a sensory invitation.

Slowly, he cautioned himself. Take it slowly. Show her how precious, how perfect, how uniquely special she is. He brushed a line of butterfly kisses over her temples, tasted the warm flush of her cheeks, closed her fluttering lashes with a soft flick of his tongue on her eyelids, trailed his lips down her nose. Her mouth was waiting for him, eager, passionate, burning.

He fought the intense wave of desire she stirred. He lifted her and carried her into the bathroom, turning on the taps in the shower and testing the temperature of the water before stepping in and letting her legs slide down his to stand again.

The sensual pleasure of soaping her all over was worth the restraint he imposed on himself, but when she took the soap and did the same for him his excitement was difficult to contain. There was a quick flurry of towelling each other dry, urgency mounting for the absolute intimacy they both craved.

Bedroom...Jayne sprawling in wild abandonment on the bed, blatantly provocative, wanting him, her arms outstretched in welcome. He lowered himself between the open invitation of her long, beautiful legs. Her hands raked his back, dragging his body to close the gap between them. 'Now?' he cried, the hot moistness of her drawing him inexorably on, shaking his control.

'Yes...yes...' Her head threshing, hair tumbling in fiery disarray around her passionate face, her legs wrapping around him, urging, cocooning him in sweet ecstacy as he thrust forward, plunging through the pulsing sheath to the innermost heart of her womanhood, feeling the soft creamy spill of her climax, the rippling sigh of fulfilment as her muscles contracted, closing around him, holding him deeply inside her.

Dan gathered her to him, capturing this perfect moment of reunion in a body-imprinting embrace, in a kiss that heightened the exquisite intimacy of melding together again. 'I love you, Jayne. With all that I am, I love you,' he murmured, and the need to show her, to give her all the pleasure he could, moved him into a slow, sensual rhythm that he knew would excite continual waves of exquisite feeling.

'Oh, Dan...' A soft, melting sigh that was music to his ears.

Her thighs quivered. She languidly moved her legs up to a higher lock around him, offering him her inner self as an incitement to his pleasure, rocking with him, her hands playing sensually over his shoulders and back.

*She wanted him.*

The two years without her washed away like insignificant flotsam on a grand sea of swelling emotion that rolled toward a homeland of milk and honey. She was glorious, tantalising, enthralling, heavenly. Dan knew he would never have enough of her, however long they lived. She called to him like some magical, elemental being that stroked every instinctive chord within him. The touch of her, the feel of her, the scent of her, he knew them all as essential parts of himself, and he marvelled at the power of nature that instinct could supersede knowledge.

He had loved her without really knowing her, yet knowing her enriched the love a thousandfold. He felt his body flood with urgent need, quicken to the pace of free-bolting desire, and she arched underneath him, *wanting him*, and he released the essence of himself deep inside her, spasmic bursts of the seeds of his whole genetic history, searching for their complement in her.

And the giving flowing from her told him it was all right now, told him she wanted their child, too, that this was a moment of total bonding, of creation, of starting anew, of opening up a new life of sharing in ways they had never explored before.

She moved with him, keeping the sealing of the bond intact as he shifted his weight, rolling them both onto their sides. He wanted to hold her so closely, so tightly that their entire bodies would meld and they would become as one, never to be separated again.

He wanted to tell her his thoughts, wanted her to know how much had changed for him, the perceptions that had opened up, making him see what he'd been missing.

He touched her lips. 'I'll always listen to your voice, Jayne. Will you forgive me my arrogance, and for everything I've done wrong?'

'If you forgive me my silence,' she answered, her hand pressing against his heart in need for his understanding.

'It's behind us,' he murmured, having no doubt it was true.

'Yes.' It was a blissful breath of unshadowed happiness.

He trailed his fingertips adoringly around her face. 'I thought the world was the ultimate experience of life, Jayne. I know now that isn't true. It offers a vista of different societies, different environments, but it cannot provide the biggest adventure of all.'

'What do you think that is, Dan?' she whispered, her eyes shining with her desire to know.

'Exploring all the wonderful facets of the people you love. You most of all, my darling. Baby Anya. And the children we'll have together. That's what belonging is all about, isn't it? That's a family. It's how we make a home.'

Tears welled into her eyes, giving them an incandescent glow. 'Yes. Oh, Dan! I love you so much.'

He cuddled her closer. 'We'll have a home, Jayne. A home of loving and sharing and contributing to each other's happiness and well-being, a home where needs are answered and dreams are pursued. I promise you I'll do my utmost to make this happen.'

'I know you will, Dan.' He was a man of his word. 'And I will, too.'

'You'll never feel lost again.'

'I know.'

'I'm here for you.'

'Yes.'

He felt her heart beating in unison with his and rested content. She was with him.

Jayne...

His wife.

His partner for life.

## CHAPTER EIGHTEEN

THE American ambassador called on them the next morning.

Jayne and Dan and Anya were enjoying a leisurely breakfast of pancakes and maple syrup, bacon and eggs and hash browns, muffins, croissants, and a selection of fruits. They had very healthy appetites. The tensions and uncertainties of yesterday were behind them. Today was the first day of a future shining with love and a new togetherness.

Their distinguished visitor did not stand on ceremony. He greeted them affably, declaring it a pleasure to meet them both. He and his aide accepted coffee and sat down with them, apparently intent on having a long, relaxed chat.

Jayne wondered if there were deplomatic repercussions over the blowing up of Sheikh Omar El Talik's Lear jet, but the ambassador did not look a worried man. Trained not to be, she thought, but refused to be worried herself. Nothing was going to dash her happiness today.

After a general discussion of current affairs in the U.S., the ambassador came to the point of his visit. 'There has been a flurry of activity along official channels regarding the events of yesterday. Not, let me hasten to add, in any way critical of your response to the action taken by Omar El Talik. Your...uh...resolution to the problem has been much admired, Mr. Drayton. Indeed, applauded in many circles.'

'My wife made it work,' Dan told him with a smile at Jayne that shouted to the world how he felt about her. 'She acted with such conviction she left Omar no room to manoeuvre.'

The ambassador gave her a respectful nod. 'Many people think very highly of you, Miss Winter. The Chinese...' He smiled, as though somewhat bemused. 'Have a special name for you, I believe. Dragon Lady. Very apt in the circumstances.'

Jayne smiled back at him. 'Thank you.'

'Have we caused a political problem?' Dan asked.

'Not at all,' the ambassador hastily assured him. 'No harm whatsoever. Quite a bit of good has come out of it, in fact. New negotiations taking place. Very favourable to everyone concerned. However, I have been asked to convey a message to you from Omar's father, Sheikh Abdul El Talik.'

'The old man is not happy with his son?' Dan observed dryly.

The ambassador sighed. 'An understatement, Mr. Drayton. Sheikh Abdul was hoping to...uh...rehabilitate his younger son from various dissolute habits he had fallen into. Give

him responsibilities appropriate to his status.
Make him prove himself worthy of the position
he inherited from his uncle. Omar was entrusted
with the task of gaining your services, Mr.
Drayton. He did not wish to confess failure to
his father. It was a matter of pride, you
understand.'

'A man has to know when to take no for an
answer,' Dan said sternly, totally unsympathetic
to any mitigating plea on Omar's behalf.

'He threatened to shoot us,' Jayne put in for
good measure.

'There is no question that Omar overstepped
all normal boundaries in trying to prove himself
effective,' the ambassador acknowledged.
'Sheikh Abdul is anxious to make amends for
the...uh...pain his son caused you. Very generous amends.'

He paused, coughed delicately, then added,
'You may or may not be aware that we, the U.S.
government, have an interest in Sheikh Abdul's
mining operations. It could be politically advan-
tageous if you could find it in your heart to accept
his offer, Mr. Drayton.' He shot a deferential
smile at Jayne. 'And Miss Winter, of course.'

'What's the offer?' Dan asked.

'Three times your previously negotiated fee for
the contract, free use of his hunting palace for
the duration of the contract with absolute guarantees of every service and security you require,

plus the unencumbered gift of a house in
London. A very fashionable address, I believe.'

'A house?' Jayne repeated incredulously.

'Sheikh Abdul owns several properties in
London, Miss Winter. Investments.'

'My wife does not have happy memories of her
last stay in the Middle East,' Dan said firmly. 'I
would not agree to anything that would make my
wife unhappy.'

'Darling, if Sheikh Abdul is prepared to keep
his son, Omar, well away from us, I can be very
happy with you in his hunting palace,' Jayne assured him, then couldn't help grinning from ear
to ear. 'It would be lovely to own a house.'

Dan looked surprised. 'I thought you were set
on establishing a home is Australia.'

'You and I can make a home for our family
anywhere,' Jayne answered with sublime confidence in their new partnership. 'If you think it's
best for us to take up Sheikh Abdul's contract
and mend political fences, that's fine by me.'

He paused to consider. 'There is Monty's
offer,' he reminded her.

'I don't know how you feel about that,' Jayne
answered cautiously, not wanting to make him
feel pinned down.

He grinned. 'We'll talk about it.' He turned to
the ambassador. 'Tell Sheikh Abdul we'll give his
deal our deepest consideration. It's obviously in
everybody's interests to have a happy resolution

that is beneficial to all of us. I would expect your people to make sure the paperwork is iron-tight.'

'You can count on that, Mr. Drayton.' The ambassador and his aide stood to shake hands and take their leave of them. 'We'll be in touch.'

His visit reminded Jayne of Chunz's part in yesterday's drama. Lin Zhiyong had told them Chunz had been safely returned to her husband and son, but Jayne felt the little Chinese woman needed to be reassured that she had not let Dan down in any way whatsoever over looking after Anya.

'We should give Chunz something, Dan. Even though it wasn't her fault, she'll still feel devastated that the kidnap happened while Anya was in her care.'

'What do you suggest?'

She thought out loud. 'Chunz probably wouldn't accept anything for herself. She'd feel wrong about it. Perhaps, even be insulted. There'd be a lot of face involved.'

'Truc,' Dan agreed.

'I know!' Jayne cried excitedly. 'Chunz is so proud of her son. He's eleven and this year he started on computers at school. Chunz has great hopes for him because he's very clever at it. Could we buy him a personal computer? It would give him an enormous advantage.'

'That's a brilliant idea, darling! No Chinese parent would refuse something that benefits their child.'

Jayne glowed under Dan's admiration. She wasn't quite so bad at people skills, after all. She didn't think she ever would be again. Having confidence in oneself made an enormous difference.

Dan suggested that the gift-giving could wait until tomorrow. The hotel manager had warned them there was a lot of media interest in their story and they decided a day secluded in their suite was a good idea. Anya's afternoon nap gave them the opportunity to take a leisurely rest themselves, although not much resting was done. The exercise, however, was intensely satisfying and wonderfully relaxing.

It was fortunate that Anya awoke when she did, because soon afterward Lin Zhiyong was announced as a visitor. He entered their suite with his usual entourage to inform them that he had arranged with the hotel to hold his ten-course duck dinner in a private banquet room, and he hoped they would still be his honoured guests this evening.

Jayne and Dan duly attended, dressed in entirely new and appropriate outfits from a selection of clothes sent up to them from the hotel boutiques.

The first course was made up of a cold platter with various cuts of duck cooked in a dark soy sauce. Jayne didn't care to identify anything too closely. Dan ate with gusto and appreciation. He always did.

The pièce de résistance was supposedly the skin of the duck which was roasted to perfection. It was dipped in a sweet-salty soy sauce and wrapped in a pancake. The meat was stir-fried with noodles, the wings braised. Other bits were fried with a variety of vegetables. The bones were made into a clear soup. Jayne was somewhat relieved that dessert did not include duck in any form.

Although the banquet was something of an endurance test, Jayne did enjoy it. It was a rare pleasure to see Lin Zhiyong in such obvious good spirits. He was a very happy Buddha tonight, his enigmatic face completely cast aside. Dan, of course, did his habitual trick of drawing everyone out and, all in all, it was a grand party.

Lin Zhiyong capped the evening with a speech.

'It has been decided that in Denjing a special house and garden will be built in honour of Mr. Drayton and his wife, Miss Winter. This is to be a home that will always be held ready to receive them and their family, welcoming them whenever they return to visit China. Today they have been made honorary citizens of our great new city.'

From having no house at all to having two houses offered as gifts to them in one day certainly called for celebration. Jayne and Dan were feeling very pleasantly merry when they returned to their suite.

As they entered the sitting room, the telephone rang. It was Monty Castle calling from Australia, wanting a firsthand account of what he'd been hearing on news bulletins. Dan explained how the situation with Omar El Talik had developed and led up to yesterday's drama.

'What's this about you and Jayne being married?' Monty demanded to know.

'We were married before Jayne came to work for you, Monty. Our marriage went through a bad patch but now we're back together again. No more separations.' His eyes seared Jayne's with that conviction.

'All the more reason to accept the partnership deal. Settle down,' Monty urged.

'We'll discuss that in another couple of months, Monty. Jayne and I think we should take up the deal with Sheikh Abdul El Talik first. However, if Jayne approves, I'd be happy to take up the partnership, although not on a gift basis. I'd rather buy my shareholding fair and square.'

'That's not necessary,' Monty argued. 'You're worth your weight in gold as it is.'

'I'll do it my way or not at all, Monty. And only if it's what Jayne wants, too.'

'Jayne wants a house. That's what she was working for. Tell her I'll throw in a house as her bonus for finishing up the Denjing contract. That'll settle things.'

*Three* houses! Jayne shook her head in incredulous amazement. She had heard of disasters coming in threes. Did dreams come true in threes?

She vaguely heard Dan finishing the conversation with Monty. Then he was turning her into his arms, smiling broadly, his eyes dancing with teasing mischief.

'Well, my love. Do you fancy putting roots down in Britain, China, Australia, or somewhere else? At the rate we're going, we could grow a forest over at least three continents.'

Jayne laughed, feeling giddily intoxicated from wine, events tumbling over each other, and most of all, the wonderful closeness to Dan. 'Maybe we should collect some more options first. Do you think the ambassador might offer us a house in the U.S.?'

Dan's arms trapped her lower body against his, swaying in a dance as old as the legends of mankind. 'For Dragon Lady, anything is possible.'

She linked her hands behind his neck and leaned back, arching her body in provocative incitement. 'Only because one day a determined warrior found his way to her lair and blew up the mountain to set her free.'

Dan smiled, his head bending toward hers. 'It had to be so,' he murmured, his mouth coming closer and closer. 'Dragons are powers of the air, and in Chinese mythology they represent the principle of heaven. More than anything else, the warrior wanted the heaven she could give him.'

Then his lips brushed hers and there was the fire of desire, the sweet air of freedom from all barriers, and the heaven of knowing they had come home to each other.

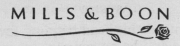

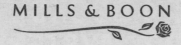

# MILLS & BOON

For those long, hot, lazy days this summer
Mills & Boon are delighted to bring you...

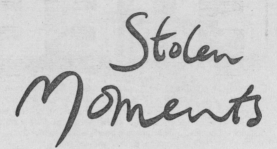

**A collection of four short sizzling stories
in one romantic volume.**

We know you'll love these warm and sensual
stories from some of our best loved authors.

| | |
|---|---|
| *Love Me Not* | Barbara Stewart |
| *Maggie And Her Colonel* | Merline Lovelace |
| *Prairie Summer* | Alina Roberts |
| *Anniversary Waltz* | Anne Marie Duquette |

'Stolen Moments' is the perfect summer read for
those stolen summer moments!

Available: June '96          Price: £4.99

*Available from WH Smith, John Menzies, Volume One, Forbuoys, Martins,
Woolworths, Tesco, Asda, Safeway and other paperback stockists.*

# GET 4 BOOKS
# AND A MYSTERY GIFT

Return this coupon and we'll send you 4 Mills & Boon Romances and a mystery gift absolutely FREE! We'll even pay the postage and packing for you.

We're making you this offer to introduce you to the benefits of Reader Service: FREE home delivery of brand-new Mills & Boon Romances, at least a month before they are available in the shops, FREE gifts and a monthly Newsletter packed with information.

Accepting these FREE books and gift places you under no obligation to buy, you may cancel at any time, even after receiving just your free shipment. Simply complete the coupon below and send it to:

MILLS & BOON READER SERVICE, FREEPOST, CROYDON, SURREY, CR9 3WZ.

## No stamp needed

Yes, please send me 4 free Mills & Boon Romances and a mystery gift. I understand that unless you hear from me, I will receive 6 superb new titles every month for just £2.10* each postage and packing free. I am under no obligation to purchase any books and I may cancel or suspend my subscription at any time, but the free books and gifts will be mine to keep in any case. (I am over 18 years of age)

1EP6R

Ms/Mrs/Miss/Mr _____

Address _____

_____

_____ Postcode _____

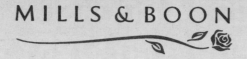

# MILLS & BOON

## Next Month's Romances

Each month you can choose from a wide variety of romance with Mills & Boon. Below are the new titles to look out for next month.

| | |
|---|---|
| ONLY BY CHANCE | Betty Neels |
| THE MORNING AFTER | Michelle Reid |
| THE DESERT BRIDE | Lynne Graham |
| THE RIGHT CHOICE | Catherine George |
| FOR THE LOVE OF EMMA | Lucy Gordon |
| WORKING GIRL | Jessica Hart |
| THE LADY'S MAN | Stephanie Howard |
| THE BABY BUSINESS | Rebecca Winters |
| WHITE LIES | Sara Wood |
| THAT MAN CALLAHAN! | Catherine Spencer |
| FLIRTING WITH DANGER | Kate Walker |
| THE BRIDE'S DAUGHTER | Rosemary Gibson |
| SUBSTITUTE ENGAGEMENT | Jayne Bauling |
| NOT PART OF THE BARGAIN | Susan Fox |
| THE PERFECT MAN | Angela Devine |
| JINXED | Day Leclaire |